Dear Reader,

It is a great pleasure for me to congratulate Silhouette Books on its 20th anniversary. I signed my first book contract with Silhouette in 1980. We go back quite a long way together, and it has been a wonderful association. All of us at Silhouette—authors, editors, artists, copy editors, salespeople, publicists and management—are a team. We work together to produce the books which our readers have so loyally purchased all these years.

Before I started writing for Silhouette Books, I was holding down a full-time job as a newspaper reporter, on call twenty-four hours a day. I did feature material for two other newspapers, as well. At night I wrote books and hoped that someday, someone would want to publish them. Sure enough, in 1980, Silhouette Books decided that I just might suit them. We entered into a partnership. Since they took me on trust, I worked very hard to earn my place as one of their authors.

Each year meant a new book, often many more than one. I can go through the titles of my books, and remember the birth of our son, Blayne, the death of both my parents, the purchase of our first and only home, my husband James's two open-heart surgeries, our son's school days and graduation, the wonderful years of my marriage and the trips to faraway places which I used to dream of seeing when I was a little girl growing up on a sharecropper's farm in southwest Georgia. I can see my life through the pages of the books I wrote during those years, and revisit warm and sweet memories of people now dead who meant so much to me when I was young and bright with ambition and dreams of publication.

I have had a wonderful career and a wonderful life. God has blessed me with a loving family, many great friends (Especially you, Ann!), the best editors on earth and a way to contribute something to the world which has given me so much. I hope that my books have helped some of you through bad times in your own lives, just as the authors I collect and love have comforted me during the storms of my own life. I wish you continued success, Silhouette Books, and I hope to remain a part of your family until I die or you get tired of me—whichever comes first. Thank you for giving me a chance to do what I love best in all the world. God bless you.

Love to Silhouette and to my very special readers,

Diana Palmer

Dear Reader,

It's going to be a wonderful year! After all, we're celebrating Silhouette's 20th anniversary of bringing you compelling, emotional, contemporary romances month after month.

January's fabulous lineup starts with beloved author Diana Palmer, who returns to Special Edition with *Matt Caldwell: Texas Tycoon.* In the latest installment of her wildly popular LONG, TALL TEXANS series, temperatures rise and the stakes are high when a rugged tycoon meets his match in an innocent beauty—who is also his feisty employee.

Bestselling author Susan Mallery continues the next round of the series PRESCRIPTION: MARRIAGE with *Their Little Princess.* In this heart-tugging story, baby doctor Kelly Hall gives a suddenly single dad lessons in parenting—and learns all about romance!

Reader favorite Pamela Toth launches Special Edition's newest series, SO MANY BABIES—in which babies and romance abound in the Buttonwood Baby Clinic. In *The Baby Legacy,* a sperm-bank mix-up brings two unlikely parents together temporarily—or perhaps forever....

In Peggy Webb's passionate story, *Summer Hawk,* two Native Americans put aside their differences when they unite to battle a medical crisis and find that love cures all. Rounding off the month is veteran author Pat Warren's poignant, must-read secret baby story, *Daddy by Surprise,* and Jean Brashear's *Lonesome No More,* in which a reclusive hero finds healing for his heart when he offers a single mom and her young son a haven from harm.

I hope you enjoy these six unforgettable romances and help us celebrate Silhouette's 20th anniversary all year long!

Best,

Karen Taylor Richman
Senior Editor

Please address questions and book requests to:
Silhouette Reader Service
U.S.: 3010 Walden Have., P.O. Box 1325, Buffalo, NY 14269
Canadian: P.O. Box 609, Fort Erie, Ont. L2A 5X3

DIANA PALMER

MATT CALDWELL: TEXAS TYCOON

Silhouette®

SPECIAL EDITION®

Published by Silhouette Books

America's Publisher of Contemporary Romance

To Eldarador and W.G. with love

SILHOUETTE BOOKS

ISBN 0-373-24297-2

MATT CALDWELL: TEXAS TYCOON

Copyright © 2000 by Diana Palmer

Visit us at www.romance.net

Printed in U.S.A.

Diana Palmer is legendary for her unforgettable tales about those lovable Long, Tall Texans...

The Long, Tall Texans series

Silhouette Romance

Calhoun #580
Justin #592
Tyler #604
Sutton's Way #670
Ethan #694
Connal #741
Harden #783
Evan #819
Donavan #843
Emmett #910
Regan's Pride #1000
Coltrain's Proposal #1103
The Princess Bride #1282
Callaghan's Bride #1355

Silhouette Desire

The Case of the Missing Secretary #733
That Burke Man #913
Beloved #1189

Silhouette Special Edition

Matt Caldwell: Texas Tycoon #1297

Silhouette Books

Abduction and Seduction 1995
"Redbird"
Lone Star Christmas 1997
"Christmas Cowboy"
A Long, Tall Texan Summer 1997
Love with a Long, Tall Texan 1999

Harlequin Books

Husbands on Horseback 1996
"Paper Husband"

DIANA PALMER got her start in writing as a newspaper reporter and published her first romance novel for Silhouette Books in 1982. In 1993, she celebrated the publication of her fiftieth novel for Silhouette Books. *Affaire de Coeur* lists her as one of the top ten romance authors in the country. Beloved by fans worldwide, Diana Palmer is the winner of numerous national Waldenbooks Romance Bestseller awards and national B. Dalton Books Bestseller awards.

IT'S OUR 20th ANNIVERSARY!
We'll be celebrating all year, starting with these fabulous titles, on sale in January 2000.

Special Edition

#1297 Matt Caldwell: Texas Tycoon
Diana Palmer

#1298 Their Little Princess
Susan Mallery

#1299 The Baby Legacy
Pamela Toth

#1300 Summer Hawk
Peggy Webb

#1301 Daddy by Surprise
Pat Warren

#1302 Lonesome No More
Jean Brashear

Intimate Moments

#979 Murdock's Last Stand
Beverly Barton

#980 Marrying Mike... Again
Alicia Scott

#981 A Drive-By Wedding
Terese Ramin

#982 Midnight Promises
Eileen Wilks

#983 The Comeback of Con MacNeill
Virginia Kantra

#984 Witness... and Wife?
Kate Stevenson

Romance

BREWSTER BABY BOOM **#1420 The Baby Bequest**
Susan Meier

#1421 With a Little T.L.C.
Teresa Southwick

#1422 The Sheik's Solution
Barbara McMahon

#1423 Annie and the Prince
Elizabeth Harbison

#1424 A Babe in the Woods
Cara Colter

#1425 Prim, Proper... Pregnant
Alice Sharpe

Desire

MAN OF THE MONTH **#1267 Her Forever Man**
Leanne Banks

#1268 The Pregnant Princess
Anne Marie Winston

#1269 Dr. Mommy
Elizabeth Bevarly

TEXAS BRIDES **#1270 Hard Lovin' Man**
Peggy Moreland

The Bridal Bid **#1271 The Cowboy Takes a Bride**
Cathleen Galitz

#1272 Skyler Hawk: Lone Brave
Sheri WhiteFeather

Chapter One

The man on the hill sat on his horse with elegance and grace, and the young woman found herself staring at him. He was obviously overseeing the roundup, which the man at her side had brought her to view. This ranch was small by Texas standards, but around Jacobsville, it was big enough to put its owner in the top ten in size.

"Dusty, isn't it?" Ed Caldwell asked with a chuckle, oblivious to the distant mounted rider, who was behind him and out of his line of sight. "I'm glad I work for the corporation and not here. I like my air cool and unpolluted."

Leslie Murry smiled. She wasn't pretty. She had a plain, rather ordinary sort of face with blond hair that had a natural wave, and gray eyes. Her one good feature besides her slender figure was a pretty bow mouth. She had a quiet, almost reclusive demeanor these days. But she hadn't always been like that. In her early teens, Leslie had been flamboyant and outgoing, a live wire of a girl whose friends had laughed at her exploits. Now, at twenty-three, she was as sedate as a matron. The change in her was shocking to people who'd once known her. She knew Ed Caldwell from college in Houston. He'd graduated in her sophomore year, and she'd quit the following semester to go to work as a paralegal for his father's law firm in Houston. Things had gotten too complicated there, and Ed had come to the rescue once again. In fact, Ed was the reason she'd just been hired as an executive assistant by the mammoth Caldwell firm. His cousin owned it.

She'd never met Mather Gilbert Caldwell, or Matt as he was known locally. People said he was a nice, easygoing man who loved an underdog. In fact, Ed said it frequently himself. They were down here for roundup so that Ed could introduce Leslie to the head of the corporation. But so far, all they'd seen was dust and cattle and hardworking cowboys.

"Wait here," Ed said. "I'm going to ride over and find Matt. Be right back." He urged his horse into a trot and held on for dear life. Leslie had to bite her lip to conceal a smile at the way he rode. It was painfully obvious that he was much more at home behind the wheel of a car. But she wouldn't have been so rude as to have mentioned it, because Ed was the only friend she had these days. He was, in fact, the only person around who knew about her past.

While she was watching him, the man on horseback on the hill behind them was watching her. She sat on a horse with style, and she had a figure that would have attracted a connoisseur of women—which the man on horseback was. Impulsively he spurred his horse into a gallop and came down the rise behind her. She didn't hear him until he reined in and the harsh sound of the horse snorting had her whirling in the saddle.

The man was wearing working clothes, like the other cowboys, but all comparisons ended there. He wasn't ragged or missing a tooth or unshaven. He was oddly intimidating, even in the way he sat the horse, with one hand on the reins and the other on his powerful denim-clad thigh.

Matt Caldwell met her gray eyes with his dark ones and noted that she wasn't the beauty he'd expected, despite her elegance of carriage and that perfect figure. "Ed brought you, I gather," he said curtly.

She'd almost guessed from his appearance that his voice would be deep and gravelly, but not that it would cut like a knife. Her hands tightened on the reins. "I…yes, he…he brought me."

The stammer was unexpected. Ed's usual sort of girl was brash and brassy, much more sophisticated than this shrinking violet here. He liked to show off Matt's ranch and impress the girls. Usually it didn't bother Matt, but he'd had a frustrating day and he was out of humor. He scowled. "Interested in cattle ranching, are you?" he drawled with ice dripping from every syllable. "We could always get you a rope and let you try your hand, if you'd like."

She felt as if every muscle in her body had gone taut. "I...came to meet Ed's cousin," she managed. "He's rich." The man's dark eyes flashed and she flushed. She couldn't believe she'd made such a remark to a stranger. "I mean," she corrected, "he owns the company where Ed works. Where I work," she added. She could have bitten her tongue for her artless mangling of a straightforward subject, but the man rattled her.

Something kindled in the man's dark eyes under the jutting brow; something not very nice at all. He leaned forward and his eyes narrowed. "Why are you really out here with Ed?" he asked.

She swallowed. He had her hypnotized, like a cobra with a rabbit. Those eyes...those very dark, unyielding eyes...!

"It's not your business, is it?" she asked finally, furious at her lack of cohesive thought and this man's assumption that he had the right to interrogate her.

He didn't say a word. Instead, he just looked at her.

"Please," she bit off, hunching her shoulders uncomfortably. "You're making me nervous!"

"You came to meet the boss, didn't you?" he asked in a velvety smooth tone. "Didn't anyone tell you that he's no marshmallow?"

She swallowed. "They say he's a very nice, pleasant man," she returned a little belligerently. "Something I'll bet nobody in his right mind would dream of saying about you!" she added with her first burst of spirit in years.

His eyebrows lifted. "How do you know I'm not nice and pleasant?" he asked, chuckling suddenly.

"You're like a cobra," she said uneasily.

He studied her for a few seconds before he nudged his horse in the side with a huge dusty boot and eased so close to her that she actually shivered. He hadn't been impressed with the young woman who stammered and stuttered with nerves, but a spirited woman was a totally new proposition. He liked a woman who wasn't intimidated by his bad mood.

His hand went across her hip to catch the back of her saddle and he looked into her eyes from an unnervingly close distance. "If I'm a cobra, then what does that make you, cupcake?" he drawled with deliberate sensuality, so close that she caught the faint smoky scent of his breath, the hint of spicy cologne that clung to his lean, tanned face. "A soft, furry little bunny?"

She was so shaken by the proximity of him that she tried desperately to get away, pulling so hard on the reins that her mount unexpectedly reared and she went down on the ground, hard, hitting her injured left hip and her shoulder as she fell into the thick grass.

A shocked sound came from the man, who vaulted out of the saddle and was beside her as she tried to sit up. He reached for her a little roughly, shaken by her panic. Women didn't usually try to back away from him; especially ordinary ones like this. She fell far short of his usual companions.

She fought his hands, her eyes huge and overly bright, panic in the very air around her. "No...!" she cried out helplessly.

He froze in place, withdrawing his lean hand from her arm, and stared at her with scowling curiosity.

"Leslie!" came a shout from a few yards away. Ed bounced up as quickly as he could manage it without being unseated. He fumbled his way off the horse and knelt beside her, holding out his arm so that she could catch it and pull herself up.

"I'm sorry," she said, refusing to look at the man who was responsible for her tumble. "I jerked the reins. I didn't mean to."

"Are you all right?" Ed asked, concerned.

She nodded. "Sure." But she was shaking, and both men could see it.

Ed glanced over her head at the taller, darker, leaner man who stood with his horse's reins in his hand, staring at the girl.

"Uh, have you two introduced yourselves?" he asked awkwardly.

Matt was torn by conflicting emotions, the strongest of which was bridled fury at the woman's panicky attitude. She acted as if he had plans to assault her, when he'd only been trying to help her up. He was angry and it cost him his temper. "The next time you bring a certifiable lunatic to my ranch, give me some advance warning," the tall man sniped at Ed. He moved as curtly as he spoke, swinging abruptly into the saddle to glare down at them. "You'd better take her home," he told Ed. "She's a damned walking liability around animals."

"But she rides very well, usually," Ed protested. "Okay, then," he added when the other man glowered at him. He forced a smile. "I'll see you later."

The tall man jerked his hat down over his eyes, wheeled the horse without another word and rode back up on the rise where he'd been sitting earlier.

"Whew!" Ed laughed, sweeping back his light brown hair uneasily. "I haven't seen him in a mood like that for years. I can't imagine what set him off. He's usually the soul of courtesy, especially when someone's hurt."

Leslie brushed off her jeans and looked up at her friend morosely. "He rode right up to me," she said unsteadily, "and leaned across me to talk with a hand on the saddle. I just…panicked. I'm sorry. I guess he's some sort of foreman here. I hope you don't get in trouble with your cousin because of it."

"That *was* my cousin, Leslie," he said heavily.

She stared at him vacantly. "That was Matt Caldwell?"

He nodded.

She let out a long breath. "Oh, boy. What a nice way to start a new job, by alienating the man at the head of the whole food chain."

"He doesn't know about you," he began.

Her eyes flashed. "And you're not to tell him," she returned firmly. "I mean it! I will not have my past paraded out again. I came down here to get away from reporters and movie producers, and that's what I'm going to do. I've had my hair cut, bought new clothes, gotten contact lenses. I've done everything I can think of so I won't be recognized. I'm not going to have it all dragged up again. It's been six years," she added miserably. "Why can't people just leave it alone?"

"The newsman was just following a lead," he said gently. "One of the men who attacked you was arrested for drunk driving and someone connected the name to your mother's case. His father is some high city official in Houston. It was inevitable that the press would dig up his son's involvement in your mother's case in an election year."

"Yes, I know, and that's what prompted the producer to think it would make a great TV movie of the week." She ground her teeth together. "That's just what we all need. And I thought it was all over. How silly of me," she said in a defeated tone. "I wish I were rich and famous," she added. "Then maybe I could buy myself some peace and privacy." She glanced up where the tall man sat silently watching the herding below. "I made some stupid remarks to your cousin, too, not knowing who he really was. I guess he'll be down in personnel first thing Monday to have me fired."

"Over my dead body," he said. "I may be only a lowly cousin, but I do own stock in the corporation. If he fires you, I'll fight for you."

"Would you really, for me?" she asked solemnly.

He ruffled her short blond hair. "You're my pal," he said. "I've had a pretty bad blow of my own. I don't want to get serious about anybody ever again. But I like having you around."

She smiled sadly. "I'm glad you can act that way about me. I can't really bear to be..." She swallowed. "I don't like men close to me, in any physical way. The therapist said I might be able to change that someday, with the right man. I don't know. It's been so long..."

"Don't sit and worry," he said. "Come on. I'll take you back to town and buy you a nice vanilla ice-cream cone. How's that?"

She smiled at him. "Thanks, Ed."

He shrugged. "Just another example of my sterling character." He glanced up toward the rise and away again. "He's just not himself today," he said. "Let's go."

Matt Caldwell watched his visitors bounce away on their respective horses with a resentment and fury he hadn't experienced in years. The little blond icicle had made him feel like a lecher. As if she could have appealed to him, a man who had movie stars chasing after him! He let out a rough sigh and pulled a much-used cigar from his pocket and stuck it in his teeth. He didn't light it. He was trying to give up the bad habit, but it was slow going. This cigar had been just recently the target of his secretary's newest weapon in her campaign to save him from nicotine. The end was still damp, in fact, despite the fact that he'd only arrived here from his office in town about an hour ago. He took it out of his mouth with a sigh, eyed it sadly and put it away. He'd threatened to fire her and she'd threatened to quit. She was a nice woman, married with two cute little kids. He couldn't let her leave him. Better the cigar than good help, he decided.

He let his eyes turn again toward the couple growing smaller in the distance. What an odd girlfriend Ed had latched onto this time. Of course, she'd let Ed touch her. She'd flinched away from Matt as if he was contagious. The more he thought about it, the madder he got. He turned his horse toward the bawling cattle in the distance. Working might take the edge off his temper.

Ed took Leslie to her small apartment at a local boardinghouse and left her at the front door with an apology.

"You don't think he'll fire me?" she asked in a plaintive tone.

He shook his head. "No," he assured her. "I've

already told you that I won't let him. Now stop worrying. Okay?"

She managed a smile. "Thanks again, Ed."

He shrugged. "No problem. See you Monday."

She watched him get into his sports car and roar away before she went inside to her lonely room at the top corner of the house, facing the street. She'd made an enemy today, without meaning to. She hoped it wasn't going to adversely affect her life. There was no going back now.

Monday morning, Leslie was at her desk five minutes early in an attempt to make a good impression. She liked Connie and Jackie, the other two women who shared administrative duties for the vice president of marketing and research. Leslie's job was more routine. She kept up with the various shipments of cattle from one location to another, and maintained the herd records. It was exacting, but she had a head for figures and she enjoyed it.

Her immediate boss was Ed, so it was really a peachy job. They had an entire building in downtown Jacobsville, a beautiful old Victorian mansion, which Matt had painstakingly renovated to use as his corporation's headquarters. There were two floors of offices, and a canteen for coffee breaks where the kitchen and dining room once had been.

Matt wasn't in his office much of the time. He did a lot of traveling, because aside from his business interests, he sat on boards of directors of other businesses and even on the board of trustees of at least one college. He had business meetings in all sorts of places. Once he'd even gone to South America to see about investing in a growing cattle market there, but he'd come home angry and disillusioned when he saw the slash and burn method of pasture creation that had already killed a substantial portion of rain forest. He wanted no part of that, so he turned to Australia instead and bought another huge ranching tract in the Northern Territory there.

Ed told her about these fascinating exploits, and Leslie listened with her eyes wide. It was a world she'd never known. She and her mother, at the best of times, had been poor before the tragedy that separated them. Now, even with Leslie's job and the good salary she made, it still meant budgeting to the bone so that she could afford even a taxi to work and pay rent on the small apartment where she lived. There wasn't much left over for travel. She envied Matt being able to get on a plane—his own private jet, in fact—and go anywhere in the world he liked. It was a glimpse inside a world she'd never know.

"I guess he goes out a lot," she murmured once when Ed had told her that his cousin was away in New York for a cattlemen's banquet.

"With women?" Ed chuckled. "He beats them off with a stick. Matt's one of the most hunted bachelors in south Texas, but he never seems to get serious about any one woman. They're just accessories to him, pretty things to take on the town. You know," he added with a faint smile, "I don't think he really likes women very much. He was kind to a couple of local girls who needed a shoulder to cry on, but that was as far as it went, and they weren't the sort of women to chase him. He's like this because he had a rough time as a child."

"How?" she asked.

"His mother gave him away when he was six."

Her intake of breath was audible. "Why?"

"She had a new boyfriend who didn't like kids," he said bluntly. "He wouldn't take Matt, so she gave him to my dad. He was raised with me. That's why we're so close."

"What about his father?" she asked.

"We...don't talk about his father."

"Ed!"

He grimaced. "This can't go any further," he said. "Okay."

"We don't think his mother knew who his father was," he confided. "There were so many men in her life around that time."

"But her husband..."

"What husband?" he asked.

She averted her eyes. "Sorry. I assumed that she was married."

"Not Beth," he mused. "She didn't want ties. She didn't want Matt, but her parents had a screaming fit when she mentioned an abortion. They wanted him terribly, planned for him, made room for him in their house, took Beth and him in the minute he was born.''

"But you said your father raised him."

"Matt has had a pretty bad break all around. Our grandparents were killed in a car wreck, and then just a few months later, their house burned down," he added. "There was some gossip that it was intentional to collect on insurance, but nothing was ever proven. Matt was outside with Beth, in the yard, early that morning when it happened. She'd taken him out to see the roses, a pretty strange and unusual thing for her. Lucky for Matt, though, because he'd have been in the house, and would have died. The insurance settlement was enough for Beth to treat herself to some new clothes and a car. She left Matt with my dad and took off with the first man who came along." His eyes were full of remembered outrage on Matt's behalf. "Grandfather left a few shares of stock in a ranch to him, along with a small trust that couldn't be touched until Matt was twenty-one. That's the only thing that kept Beth from getting her hands on it. When he inherited it, he seemed to have an instinct for making money. He never looked back."

"What happened to his mother?" she asked.

"We heard that she died a few years ago. Matt never speaks of her."

"Poor little boy," she said aloud.

"Don't make that mistake," he said at once. "Matt doesn't need pity."

"I guess not. But it's a shame that he had to grow up so alone."

"You'd know about that."

She smiled sadly. "I guess so. My dad died years ago. Mama supported us the best way she could. She wasn't very intelligent, but she was pretty. She used what she had." Her eyes were briefly haunted. "I haven't gotten over what she did. Isn't it horrible, that in a few seconds you can destroy your own life and several other peoples' like that? And what was it all for? Jealousy, when there wasn't even a reason for it. He didn't care about me—he just wanted to have a good time with an innocent girl, him and his drunk friends." She shivered at the memory. "Mama thought she loved him. But that jealous rage didn't get him back. He died."

"I agree that she shouldn't have shot him, but it's hard to defend what he and his friends were doing to you at the time, Leslie."

She nodded. "I know," she said simply. "Sometimes kids get the short end of the stick, and it's up to them to do better with their future."

All the same, she wished that she'd had a normal upbringing, like so many other kids had.

After their conversation, she felt sorry for Matt Caldwell and wished that they'd started off better. She shouldn't have overreacted. But it was curious that he'd been so offensive to her, when Ed said that he was the soul of courtesy around women. Perhaps he'd just had a bad day.

* * *

Later in the week, Matt was back, and Leslie began to realize how much trouble she'd landed herself in from their first encounter.

He walked into Ed's office while Ed was out at a meeting, and the ice in his eyes didn't begin to melt as he watched Leslie typing away at the computer. She hadn't seen him, and he studied her with profound, if prejudiced, curiosity. She was thin and not much above average height, with short blond hair that curled toward her face. Nice skin, but she was much too pale. He remembered her eyes most of all, wide and full of distaste as he came close. It amazed him that there was a woman on the planet who could find his money repulsive, even if he didn't appeal to her himself. It was new and unpleasant to discover a woman who didn't want him. He'd never been repulsed by a woman in his life. It left him feeling inadequate. Worse, it brought back memories of the woman who'd rejected him, who'd given him away at the age of six because she didn't want him.

She felt his eyes on her and lifted her head. Gray eyes widened and stared as her hands remained suspended just over the black keyboard.

He was wearing a vested gray suit. It looked very expensive, and his eyes were dark and cutting. He had a cigar in his hand, but it wasn't lit. She hoped he wasn't going to try to smoke it in the confined space, because she was allergic to tobacco smoke.

"So you're Ed's," he murmured in that deep, cutting tone.

"Ed's assistant," she agreed. "Mr. Caldwell…"

"What did you do to land the job?" he continued with a faintly mocking smile. "And how often?"

She wasn't getting what he implied. She blinked, still staring. "I beg your pardon?"

"Why did Ed bring you in here above ten other more qualified applicants?" he persisted.

"Oh, that." She hesitated. She couldn't tell him the real reason, so she told him enough of the truth to distract him. "I have the equivalent of an associate in arts degree in business and I worked as a paralegal for his father for four years in a law office," she said. "I might not have the bachelor's degree that was preferred, but I have experience. Or so Ed assured me," she added, looking worried.

"Why didn't you finish college?" he persisted.

She swallowed. "I had…some personal problems at the time."

"You still have some personal problems, Miss Murry," he replied lazily, but his eyes were cold and alert in a lean, hard face. "You can put me at the top of the list. I had other plans for the position you're holding. So you'd better be as good as Ed says you are."

"I'll give value for money, Mr. Caldwell," she assured him. "I work for my living. I don't expect free rides."

"Don't you?"

"No, I don't."

He lifted the cigar to his mouth, looked at the wet tip, sighed and slipped it back down to dangle, unlit in his fingers.

"Do you smoke?" she asked, having noted the action.

"I try to," he murmured.

Just as he spoke, a handsome woman in her forties with blond hair in a neat bun and wearing a navy-and-white suit, walked down the hall toward him.

He glared at her as she paused in the open door of Ed's office. "I need you to sign these, Mr. Caldwell. And Mr. Bailey is waiting in your office to speak to you about that committee you want him on."

"Thanks, Edna."

Edna Jones smiled. "Good day, Miss Murry. Keeping busy, are you?"

"Yes, ma'am, thank you," Leslie replied with a genuine smile.

"Don't let him light that thing," Edna continued, gesturing toward the cigar dangling in Matt's fingers. "If you need one of these—" she held up a small water pistol "—I'll see that you get one." She smiled at a fuming Matt. "You'll be glad to know that I've already passed them out to the girls in the other executive offices, Mr. Caldwell. You can count on all of us to help you quit smoking."

Matt glared at her. She chuckled like a woman twenty years younger, waved to Leslie, and stalked off back to the office. Matt actually started to make a comical lunge after her, but caught himself in time. It wouldn't do to show weakness to the enemy.

He gave Leslie a cool glance, ignoring the faint amusement in her gray eyes. With a curt nod, he followed Edna down the hall, the damp, expensive cigar still dangling from his lean fingers.

Chapter Two

From her first day on the job, Leslie was aware of Matt's dislike and disapproval of her. He piled the work on Ed, so that it would inevitably drift down to Leslie. A lot of it was really unnecessary, like having her type up old herd records from ten years ago, which had never been converted to computer files. He said it was so that he could check progress on the progeny of his earlier herd sires, but even Ed muttered when Leslie showed him what she was expected to do.

"We have secretaries to do this sort of thing," Ed grumbled as he stared at the yellowed pages on her desk. "I need you for other projects."

"Tell him," Leslie suggested.

He shook his head. "Not in the mood he's been in lately," he said with a rueful smile. "He isn't himself."

"Did you know that his secretary is armed?" she asked suddenly. "She carries a water pistol around with her."

Ed chuckled. "Matt asked her to help him stop smoking cigars. Not that he usually did it inside the building," he was quick to add. "But Mrs. Jones feels that if you can't light a cigar, you can't smoke it. She bought a water pistol for herself and armed the other secretaries, too. If Matt even lifts a cigar to his mouth in the executive offices, they shoot him."

"Dangerous ladies," she commented.

"You bet. I've seen…"

"Nothing to do?" purred a soft, deep voice from behind Ed. The piercing dark eyes didn't match the bantering tone.

"Sorry, Matt," Ed said immediately. "I was just passing the time of day with Leslie. Can I do anything for you?"

"I need an update on that lot of cattle we placed with Ballenger," he said. He stared at Leslie with narrowed eyes. "Your job, I believe?"

She swallowed and nodded, jerking her fingers on the keyboard so that she opened the wrong file and had to push the right buttons to close it again. Normally she wasn't a nervous person, but he made her ill at ease, standing over her without speaking. Ed seemed to be a little twitchy, himself, because he moved back to his own office the minute the phone rang, placing himself out of the line of fire with an apologetic look that Leslie didn't see.

"I thought you were experienced with computers," Matt drawled mockingly as he paused beside her to look over her shoulder.

The feel of his powerful body so close behind her made every muscle tense. Her fingers froze on the keyboard, and she was barely breathing.

With a murmured curse, Matt stepped back to the side of the desk, fighting the most intense emotions he'd ever felt. He stuck his hands deep into the pockets of his slacks and glared at her.

She relaxed, but only enough to be able to pull up the file he wanted and print it for him.

He took it out of the printer tray when it was finished and gave it a slow perusal. He muttered something, and tossed the first page down on Leslie's desk.

"Half these words are misspelled," he said curtly.

She looked at it on the computer screen and nodded. "Yes, they are, Mr. Caldwell. I'm sorry, but I didn't type it."

Of course she hadn't typed it, it was ten years old, but something inside him wanted to hold her accountable for it.

He moved away from the desk as he read the rest of the pages. "You can do this file—and the others—over," he murmured as he skimmed. "The whole damned thing's illiterate."

She knew that there were hundreds of records in this particular batch of files, and that it would take days, not minutes or hours, to complete the work. But he owned the place, so he could set the rules. She pursed her lips and glanced at him speculatively. Now that he was physically out of range, she felt safe again. "Your wish is my command, boss," she murmured dryly, surprising a quick glance from him. "Shall I just put aside all of Ed's typing and devote the next few months to this?"

Her change of attitude from nervous kid to sassy woman caught him off guard. "I didn't put a time limit on it," Matt said curtly. "I only said, do it!"

"Oh, yes, sir," she agreed at once, and smiled vacantly.

He drew in a short breath and glared down at her. "You're remarkably eager to please, Miss Murry. Or is it just because I'm the boss?"

"I always try to do what I'm asked to do, Mr. Caldwell," she assured him. "Well, almost always," she amended. "Within reason."

He moved back toward the desk. As he leaned over to put down the papers she'd printed for him, he saw her visibly tense. She was the most confounding woman he'd ever known, a total mystery.

"What would you define as 'within reason'?" he drawled, holding her eyes.

She looked hunted. Amazing, that she'd been jovial and uninhibited just seconds before. Her stiff expression made him feel oddly guilty. He turned away. "Ed! Have you got my Angus file?" he called to his cousin through the open door to Ed's private office.

Ed was off the phone and he had a file folder in his hands. "Yes, sorry. I wanted to check the latest growth figures and projected weight gain ratios. I meant to put it back on your desk and I got busy."

Matt studied the figures quietly and then nodded. "That's acceptable. The Ballenger brothers do a good job."

"They're expanding, did you know?" Ed chuckled. "Nice to see them prospering."

"Yes, it is. They've worked hard enough in their lives to warrant a little prosperity."

While he spoke, Leslie was watching him covertly. She thought about the six-year-old boy whose mother had given him away, and it wrung her heart. Her own childhood had been no picnic, but Matt's upbringing had been so much worse.

He felt those soft gray eyes on his face, and his own gaze jerked down to meet them. She flushed and looked away.

He wondered what she'd been thinking to produce such a reaction. She couldn't have possibly made it plainer that she felt no physical attraction to him, so why the wide-eyed stare? It puzzled him. So many things about her puzzled him. She was neat and attractively dressed, but those clothes would have suited a dowager far better than a young woman. While he didn't encourage short skirts and low-cut blouses, Leslie was covered from head to toe; long dress, long sleeves, high neck buttoned right up to her throat.

"Need anything else?" Ed asked abruptly, hoping to ward off more trouble.

Matt's powerful shoulders shrugged. "Not for the moment." He glanced once more at Leslie. "Don't forget those files I want updated."

After he walked out, Ed stared after him for a minute, frowning. "What files?"

She explained it to him.

"But those are outdated," Ed murmured thoughtfully. "And he never looks at them. I don't understand why he has to have them corrected at all."

She leaned forward. "Because it will irritate me and make me work harder!" she said in a stage whisper. "God forbid that I should have time to twiddle my thumbs."

His eyebrows arched. "He isn't vindictive."

"That's what you think." She picked up the file Matt had left and grimaced as she put it back in the filing cabinet. "I'll start on those when I've finished answering your mail. Do you suppose he wants me to stay over after work to do them? He'd have to pay me overtime." She grinned impishly, a reminder of the woman she'd once been. "Wouldn't that make his day?"

"Let me ask him," Ed volunteered. "Just do your usual job for now."

"Okay. Thanks, Ed."

He shrugged. "What are friends for?" he murmured with a smile.

The office was a great place to work. Leslie had a ball watching the other women in the executive offices lie in wait for Matt. His secretary caught him trying to light a cigar out on the balcony, and she let him have it from behind a potted tree with the water pistol. He laid the cigar down on Bessie David's desk and she "accidentally" dropped it into his half-full coffee cup that he'd set down next to it. He held it up, dripping, with an accusing look at Bessie.

"You told me to do it, sir," Bessie reminded him.

He dropped the sodden cigar back in the coffee and left it behind. Leslie, having seen the whole thing, ducked into the rest room to laugh. It amazed her that Matt was so easygoing and friendly to his other employees. To Leslie, he was all bristle and venom. She wondered what he'd do if she let loose with a water pistol. She chuckled, imagining herself tearing up Main Street in Jacobsville ahead of a cursing Matt Caldwell. It was such a pity that she'd changed so much. Before tragedy had touched her young life, she would have been very attracted to the tall, lean cattleman.

A few days later, he came into Ed's office dangling a cigar from his fingers. Leslie, despite her amusement at the antics of the other secretaries, didn't say a word at the sight of the unlit cigar.

"I want to see the proposal the Cattlemen's Association drafted about brucellosis testing."

She stared at him. "Sir?"

He stared back. She was getting easier on his eyes, and he didn't like his reactions to her. She was repulsed by him. He couldn't get past that because it destroyed his pride. "Ed told me he had a copy of it," he elaborated. "It came in the mail yesterday."

"Okay." She knew where the mail was kept. Ed tried to ignore it, leaving it in the In box until Leslie dumped it on his desk in front of him and refused to leave until he dealt with it. This usually happened at the end of the week, when it had piled up and overflowed into the Out box.

She rummaged through the box and produced a thick letter from the Cattlemen's Association, unopened. She carried it back through and handed it to Matt.

He'd been watching her walk with curious intensity. She was limping. He couldn't see her legs, because she was wearing loose knit slacks with a tunic that flowed to her thighs as she walked. Very obviously, she wasn't going to do anything to call attention to her figure.

"You're limping," he said. "Did you see a doctor after that fall you took at my ranch?"

"No need to," she said at once. "It was only a bruise. I'm sore, that's all."

He picked up the receiver of the phone on her desk and pressed the intercom button. "Edna," he said abruptly, ''set Miss Murry up with Lou Coltrain as soon as possible. She took a spill from a horse at my place a few days ago and she's still limping. I want her X-rayed.''

''No!'' Leslie protested.

''Let her know when you've made the appointment. Thanks,'' he told his secretary and hung up. His dark eyes met Leslie's pale ones squarely. ''You're going,'' he said flatly.

She hated doctors. Oh, how she hated them! The doctor at the emergency room in Houston, an older man retired from regular practice, had made her feel cheap and dirty as he examined her and made cold remarks about tramps who got men killed. She'd never gotten over the double trauma of her experience and that harsh lecture, despite the therapists' attempts to soften the memory.

She clenched her teeth and glared at Matt. ''I said I'm not hurt!''

''You work here. I'm the boss. You get examined. Period.''

She wanted to quit. She wished she could. She had no place else to go. Houston was out of the question. She was too afraid that she'd be up to her ears in reporters, despite her physical camouflage, the minute she set foot in the city.

She drew a sharp, angry breath.

Her attitude puzzled him. ''Don't you want to make sure the injury won't make that limp permanent?'' he asked suddenly.

She lifted her chin proudly. "Mr. Caldwell, I had an...accident...when I was seventeen and that leg suffered some bone damage." She refused to think about how it had happened. "I'll always have a slight limp, and it's not from the horse throwing me."

He didn't seem to breathe for several seconds. "All the more reason for an examination," he replied. "You like to live dangerously, I gather. You've got no business on a horse."

"Ed said the horse was gentle. It was my fault I got thrown. I jerked the reins."

His eyes narrowed. "Yes, I remember. You were trying to get away from me. Apparently you think I have something contagious."

She could see the pride in his eyes that made him resent her. "It wasn't that," she said. She averted her gaze to the wall. "It's just that I don't like to be touched."

"Ed touches you."

She didn't know how to tell him without telling him everything. She couldn't bear having him know about her sordid past. She raised turbulent gray eyes to his dark ones. "I don't like to be touched by strangers," she amended quickly. "Ed and I have known each other for years," she said finally. "It's...different with him."

His eyes narrowed. He searched over her thin face. "It must be," he said flatly.

His mocking smile touched a nerve. "You're like a steamroller, aren't you?" she asked abruptly. "You assume that because you're wealthy and powerful, there isn't a woman alive who can resist you!''

He didn't like that assumption. His eyes began to glitter. ''You shouldn't listen to gossip,'' he said, his voice deadly quiet. ''She was a spoiled little debutante who thought Daddy should be able to buy her any man she wanted. When she discovered that he couldn't, she came to work for a friend of mine and spent a couple of weeks pursuing me around Jacobsville. I went home one night and found her piled up in my bed wearing a sheet and nothing else. I threw her out, but then she told everyone that I'd assaulted her. She had a field day with me in court until my housekeeper, Tolbert, was called to tell the truth about what happened. The fact that she lost the case should tell you what the jury thought of her accusations.''

''The jury?'' she asked huskily. Besides his problems with his mother, she hadn't known about any incident in his past that might predispose him even further to distrusting women.

His thin lips drew up in a travesty of a smile. ''She had me arrested and prosecuted for criminal assault,'' he returned. ''I became famous locally—the one black mark in an otherwise unremarkable past. She had the misfortune to try the same trick later on an oilman up in Houston. He called me to testify in his behalf. When he won the case, he had her prosecuted for fraud and extortion, and won. She went to jail.''

She felt sick. He'd had his own dealings with the

press. She was sorry for him. It must have been a real ordeal after what he'd already suffered in his young life. It also explained why he wasn't married. Marriage involved trust. She doubted he was capable of it any longer. Certainly it explained the hostility he showed toward Leslie. He might think she was pretending to be repulsed by him because she was playing some deep game for profit, perhaps with some public embarrassment in mind. He might even think she was setting him up for another assault charge.

"Maybe you think that I'm like that," she said after a minute, studying him quietly. "But I'm not."

"Then why act like I'm going to attack you whenever I come within five feet of you?" he asked coldly.

She studied her fingers on the desk before her, their short fingernails neatly trimmed, with a coat of colorless sheen. Nothing flashy, she thought, and that was true of her life lately. She didn't have an answer for him.

"Is Ed your lover?" he persisted coldly.

She didn't flinch. "Ask him."

He rolled the unlit cigar in his long fingers as he watched her. "You are one enormous puzzle," he mused.

"Not really. I'm very ordinary." She looked up. "I don't like doctors, especially male ones..."

"Lou's a woman," he replied. "She and her husband are both physicians. They have a little boy."

"Oh." A woman. That would make things easier. But she didn't want to be examined. They could probably tell from X rays how breaks occurred, and she didn't know if she could trust a local doctor not to talk about it.

"It isn't up to you," he said suddenly. "You work for me. You had an accident on my ranch." He smiled mirthlessly. "I have to cover my bets. You might decide later on to file suit for medical benefits."

She searched his eyes. She couldn't really blame him for feeling like that. "Okay," she said. "I'll let her examine me."

"No comment?"

She shrugged. "Mr. Caldwell, I work hard for my paycheck. I always have. You don't know me, so I don't blame you for expecting the worst. But I don't want a free ride through life."

One of his eyebrows jerked. "I've heard that one before."

She smiled sadly. "I suppose you have." She touched her keyboard absently. "This Dr. Coltrain, is she the company doctor?"

"Yes."

She gnawed on her lower lip. "What she finds out, it is confidential, isn't it?" she added worriedly, looking up at him.

He didn't reply for a minute. The hand dangling the cigar twirled it around. "Yes," he said. "It's

confidential. You're making me curious, Miss Murry.
Do you have secrets?''

"We all have secrets," she said solemnly. "Some
are darker than others.''

He flicked a thumbnail against the cigar. "What's
yours? Did you shoot your lover?''

She didn't dare show a reaction to that. Her face
felt as if it would crack if she moved.

He stuck the cigar in his pocket. "Edna will let
you know when you're to go see Lou," he said
abruptly, with a glance at his watch. He held up the
letter. "Tell Ed I've got this. I'll talk to him about
it later.''

"Yes, sir.''

He resisted the impulse to look back at her. The
more he discovered about his newest employee, the
more intrigued he became. She made him restless.
He wished he knew why.

There was no way to get out of the doctor's appointment. Leslie spoke briefly with Dr. Coltrain before she was sent to the hospital for a set of X rays.
An hour later, she was back in Lou's office, watching
the older woman pore somberly over the films
against a lighted board on the wall.

Lou looked worried when she examined the X ray
of the leg. "There's no damage from the fall, except
for some bruising," she concluded. Her dark eyes
met Leslie's squarely. "These old breaks aren't con-
sistent with a fall, however.''

Leslie ground her teeth together. She didn't say anything.

Lou moved back around her desk and sat down, indicating that Leslie should sit in the chair in front of the desk after she got off the examining table.

"You don't want to talk about it," Lou said gently. "I won't press you. You do know that the bones weren't properly set at the time, don't you? The improper alignment is unfortunate, because that limp isn't going to go away. I really should send you to an orthopedic surgeon."

"You can send me," Leslie replied, "but I won't go."

Lou rested her folded hands on her desk over the calendar blotter with its scribbled surface. "You don't know me well enough to confide in me. You'll learn, after you've been in Jacobsville a while, that I can be trusted. I don't talk about my patients to anyone, not even my husband. Matt won't hear anything from me."

Leslie remained silent. It was impossible to go over it again with a stranger. It had been hard enough to elaborate on her past to the therapist, who'd been shocked, to put it mildly.

The older woman sighed. "All right, I won't pressure you. But if you ever need anyone to talk to, I'll be here."

Leslie looked up. "Thank you," she said sincerely.

"You're not Matt's favorite person, are you?" Lou asked abruptly.

Leslie laughed without mirth. "No, I'm not. I think he'll find a way to fire me eventually. He doesn't like women much."

"Matt likes everybody as a rule," Lou said. "And he's always being pursued by women. They love him. He's kind to people he likes. He offered to marry Kitty Carson when she quit working for Dr. Drew Morris. She didn't do it, of course, she was crazy for Drew and vice versa. They're happily married now." She hesitated, but Leslie didn't speak. "He's a dish—rich, handsome, sexy, and usually the easiest man on earth to get along with."

"He's a bulldozer," Leslie said flatly. "He can't seem to talk to people unless he's standing on them." She folded her arms over her chest and looked uncomfortable.

So that's it, Lou thought, wondering if the young woman realized what her body language was giving away. Lou knew instantly that someone had caused those breaks in the younger woman's leg; very probably a man. She had reason to know.

"You don't like people to touch you," Lou said.

Leslie shifted in the chair. "No."

Lou's perceptive eyes went over the concealing garments Leslie wore, but she didn't say another word. She stood up, smiling gently. "There's no damage from the recent fall," she said gently. "But come back if the pain gets any worse."

Leslie frowned. "How did you know I was in pain?"

"Matt said you winced every time you got out of your chair."

Leslie's heart skipped. "I didn't realize he noticed."

"He's perceptive."

Lou prescribed an over-the-counter medication to take for the pain and advised her to come back if she didn't improve. Leslie agreed and went out of the office in an absentminded stupor, wondering what else Matt Caldwell had learned from her just by observation. It was a little unnerving.

When she went back to the office, it wasn't ten minutes before Matt was standing in the doorway.

"Well?" he asked.

"I'm fine," she assured him. "Just a few bruises. And believe me, I have no intention of suing you."

He didn't react visibly. "Plenty have." He was irritated. Lou wouldn't tell him anything, except that his new employee was as closemouthed as a clam. He knew that already.

"Tell Ed I'll be out of the office for a couple of days," he said.

"Yes, sir."

He gave her a last look, turned and walked back out. It wasn't until Matt was out of sight that Leslie began to relax.

Chapter Three

The nightmares came back that night. Leslie had even expected them, because of the visit to Dr. Lou Coltrain and the hospital's X-ray department. Having to wear high heeled shoes to work hadn't done her damaged leg any good, either. Along with the nightmare that left her sweating and panting, her leg was killing her. She went to the bathroom and downed two aspirin, hoping they were going to do the trick. She decided that she was going to have to give up fashion and wear flats again.

Matt noticed, of course, when he returned to the office three days later. His eyes narrowed as he watched her walk across the floor of her small office.

"Lou could give you something to take for the pain," he said abruptly.

She glanced at him as she pulled a file out of the metal cabinet. "Yes, she could, Mr. Caldwell, but do you really want a comatose secretary in Ed's office? Painkillers put me to sleep."

"Pain makes for inefficiency."

She nodded. "I know that. I have a bottle of aspirin in my purse," she assured him. "And the pain isn't so bad that I can't remember how to spell. It's just a few bruises. They'll heal. Dr. Coltrain said so."

He stared at her through narrowed, cold eyes. "You shouldn't be limping after a week. I want you to see Lou again..."

"I've limped for six years, Mr. Caldwell," she said serenely. Her eyes kindled. "If you don't like the limp, perhaps you shouldn't stand and watch me walk."

His eyebrows arched. "Can't the doctors do anything to correct it?"

She glared at him. "I hate doctors!"

The vehemence of her statement took him aback. She meant it, too. Her face flushed, her eyes sparkled with temper. It was such a difference from her usual expression that he found himself captivated. When she was animated, she was pretty.

"They're not all bad," he replied finally.

"There's only so much you can do with a shattered bone," she said and then bit her lip. She hadn't meant to tell him that.

The question was in his eyes, on his lips, but it

never made it past them. Just as he started to ask, Ed came out of his office and spotted him.

"Matt! Welcome back," he said, extending a hand. "I just had a call from Bill Payton. He wanted to know if you were coming to the banquet Saturday night. They've got a live band scheduled."

"Sure," Matt said absently. "Tell him to reserve two tickets for me. Are you going?"

"I thought I would. I'll bring Leslie along." He smiled at her. "It's the annual Jacobsville Cattlemen's Association banquet. We have speeches, but if you survive them, and the rubber chicken, you get to dance."

"Her leg isn't going to let her do much dancing," Matt said solemnly.

Ed's eyebrows lifted. "You'd be surprised," he said. "She loves Latin dances." He grinned at Leslie. "So does Matt here. You wouldn't believe what he can do with a mambo or a rhumba, to say nothing of the tango. He dated a dance instructor for several months, and he's a natural anyway."

Matt didn't reply. He was watching the play of expressions on Leslie's face and wondering about that leg. Maybe Ed knew the truth of it, and he could worm it out of him.

"You can ride in with us," Matt said absently. "I'll hire Jack Bailey's stretch limo and give your secretary a thrill."

"It'll give me a thrill, too," Ed assured him.

"Thanks, Matt. I hate trying to find a parking space at the country club when there's a party."

"That makes two of us."

One of the secretaries motioned to Matt that he had a phone call. He left and Ed departed right behind him for a meeting. Leslie wondered how she was going to endure an evening of dancing without ending up close to Matt Caldwell, who already resented her standoffish attitude. It would be an ordeal, she supposed, and wondered if she could develop a convenient headache on Saturday afternoon.

Leslie only had one really nice dress that was appropriate to wear to the function at the country club. The gown was a long sheath of shimmery silver fabric, suspended from her creamy shoulders by two little spaghetti straps. With it, she wore a silver-and-rhinestone clip in her short blond hair and neat little silver slippers with only a hint of a heel.

Ed sighed at the picture she made when the limousine pulled up in front of the boardinghouse where she was staying. She met him on the porch, a small purse clenched in damp hands, all aflutter at the thought of her first evening out since she was seventeen. She was terribly nervous.

"Is the dress okay?" she asked at once.

Ed smiled, taking in her soft oval face with its faint blush of lipstick and rouge, which was the only makeup she ever wore. Her gray eyes had naturally thick black lashes, which never needed mascara.

"You look fine," he assured her.

"You're not bad in a tux yourself," she murmured with a grin.

"Don't let Matt see how nervous you are," he said as they approached the car. "Somebody phoned and set him off just as we left my house. Carolyn was almost in tears."

"Carolyn?" she asked.

"His latest trophy girlfriend," he murmured. "She's from one of the best families in Houston, staying with her aunt so she'd be on hand for tonight's festivities. She's been relentlessly pursuing Matt for months. Some of us think she's gaining ground."

"She's beautiful, I guess?" she asked.

"Absolutely. In a way, she reminds me of Franny."

Franny had been Ed's fiancée, shot to death in a foiled bank robbery about the time Leslie had been catapulted into sordid fame. It had given them something in common that drew them together as friends.

"That must be rough," Leslie said sympathetically.

He glanced at her curiously as they approached the car. "Haven't you ever been in love?"

She shrugged, tugging the small faux fur cape closer around her shoulders. "I was a late bloomer." She swallowed hard. "What happened to me turned me right off men."

"I'm not surprised."

He waited while the chauffeur, also wearing a tuxedo, opened the door of the black super-stretch limousine for them. Leslie climbed in, followed by Ed, and the door closed them in with Matt and the most beautiful blond woman Leslie had ever seen. The other woman was wearing a simple black sheath dress with a short skirt and enough diamonds to open a jewelry store. No point in asking if they were real, Leslie thought, considering the look of that dress and the very real sable coat wrapped around it.

"You remember my cousin, Ed," Matt drawled, lounging back in the leather seat across from Ed and Leslie. Small yellow lights made it possible for them to see each other in the incredibly spacious interior. "This is his secretary, Miss Murry. Carolyn Engles," he added, nodding toward the woman at his side.

Murmured acknowledgments followed his introduction. Leslie's fascinated eyes went from the bar to the phones to the individual controls on the air-conditioning and heating systems. It was like a luxury apartment on wheels, she thought, and tried not to let her amusement show.

"Haven't you ever been in a limousine before?" Matt asked with a mocking smile.

"Actually, no," she replied with deliberate courtesy. "It's quite a treat. Thank you."

He seemed disconcerted by her reply. He averted his head and studied Ed. His next words showed he'd forgotten her. "Tomorrow morning, first thing, I want you to pull back every penny of support we're giving Marcus Boles. Nobody, and I mean nobody, involves me in a shady land deal like that!''

"It amazes me that we didn't see through him from the start,'' Ed agreed. ''The whole campaign was just a diversion, to give the real candidate someone to shoot down. He'll look like a hero, and Boles will take the fall manfully. I understand he's being handsomely paid for his disgrace. Presumably the cash is worth his reputation and social standing.''

"He's got land in South America. I hear he's going over there to live. Just as well,'' Matt added coldly. ''If he's lucky, he might make it to the airport tomorrow before I catch up with him.''

The threat of violence lay over him like an invisible mantle. Leslie shivered. Of the four people in that car, she knew firsthand how vicious and brutal physical violence could be. Her memories were hazy, confused, but in the nightmares she had constantly, they were all too vivid.

"Do calm down, darling,'' Carolyn told Matt gently. ''You're upsetting Ms. Marley.''

"Murry,'' Ed corrected before Leslie could. ''Strange, Carolyn, I don't remember your memory being so poor.''

Carolyn cleared her throat. ''It's a lovely night, at least,'' she said, changing the subject. ''No rain and a beautiful moon.''

"So it is,'' Ed drawled.

Matt gave him a cool look, which Ed met with a vacant smile. Leslie was amused by the way Ed could look so innocent. She knew him far too well to be fooled.

Matt, meanwhile, was drinking in the sight of Leslie in that formfitting dress that just matched her eyes. She had skin like marble, and he wondered if it was as soft to the touch as it seemed. She wasn't conventionally pretty, but there was a quality about her that made him weak in the knees. He was driven to protect her, without knowing why he felt that way about a stranger. It irritated him as much as the phone call he'd fielded earlier.

"Where are you from, Ms. Murbery?" Carolyn asked.

"Miss Murry," Leslie corrected, beating Ed to the punch. "I'm from a little town north of Houston."

"A true Texan," Ed agreed with a grin in her direction.

"What town?" Matt asked.

"I'm sure you won't have heard of it," Leslie said confidently. "Our only claim to fame was a radio station in a building shaped like a ten-gallon hat. Very much off the beaten path."

"Did your parents own a ranch?" he persisted.

She shook her head. "My father was a crop duster."

"A what?" Carolyn asked with a blank face.

"A pilot who sprays pesticides from the air in a small airplane," Leslie replied. "He was killed...on the job."

"Pesticides," Matt muttered darkly. "Just what the groundwater table needs to—"

"Matt, can we forget politics for just one night?" Ed asked. "I'd like to enjoy my evening."

Matt gave him a measured glare with one eye narrowed menacingly. But he relaxed all at once and leaned back in his seat, to put a lazy arm around Carolyn and let her snuggle close to him. His dark eyes seemed to mock Leslie as if comparing her revulsion to Carolyn's frank delight in his physical presence.

She let him win this round with an amused smile. Once, she might have enjoyed his presence just as much as his date was reveling in now. But she had more reason than most to fear men.

The country club, in its sprawling clubhouse on a man-made lake, was a beautiful building with graceful arches and fountains. It did Jacobsville proud. But, as Ed had intimated, there wasn't a single parking spot available. Matt had the pager number of the driver and could summon the limousine whenever it was needed. He herded his charges out of the car and into the building, where the reception committee made them welcome.

There was a live band, a very good one, playing assorted tunes, most of which resembled bossa nova rhythms. The only time that Leslie really felt alive was when she could close her eyes and listen to music; any sort of music—classical, opera, country-western or gospel. Music had been her escape as a child from a world too bitter sometimes to stomach. She couldn't play an instrument, but she could dance. That was the one thing she and her mother had shared, a love of dancing. In fact, Marie had taught her every dance step she knew, and she knew a lot. Marie had taught dancing for a year or so and had shared her expertise with her daughter. How ironic it was that Leslie's love of dance had been stifled forever by the events of her seventeenth year.

"Fill a plate," Ed coaxed, motioning her to the small china dishes on the buffet table. "You could use a little more meat on those bird bones."

She grinned at him. "I'm not skinny."

"Yes, you are," he replied, and he wasn't kidding. "Come on, forget your troubles and enjoy yourself. Tonight, there is no tomorrow. Eat, drink and be merry."

For tomorrow, you die, came the finish to that admonishing verse, she recalled darkly. But she didn't say it. She put some cheese straws and finger sandwiches on a plate and opted for soda water instead of a drink.

Ed found them two chairs on the rim of the dance floor, where they could hear the band and watch the dancing.

The band had a lovely dark-haired singer with a hauntingly beautiful voice. She was playing a guitar and singing songs from the sixties, with a rhythm that made Leslie's heart jump. The smile on her face, the sparkle in her gray eyes as she listened to the talented performer, made her come alive.

From across the room, Matt noted the abrupt change in Leslie. She loved music. She loved dancing, too, he could tell. His strong fingers contracted around his own plate.

"Shall we sit with the Devores, darling?" Carolyn asked, indicating a well-dressed couple on the opposite side of the ballroom.

"I thought we'd stick with my cousin," he said carelessly. "He's not used to this sort of thing."

"He seems very much at home," Carolyn corrected, reluctantly following in Matt's wake. "It's his date who looks out of place. Good heavens, she's tapping her toe! How gauche!"

"Weren't you ever twenty-three?" he asked with a bite in his voice. "Or were you born so damned sophisticated that nothing touched you?"

She actually gasped. Matt had never spoken to her that way.

"Excuse me," he said gruffly, having realized his mistake. "I'm still upset by Boles."

"So...so I noticed," she stammered, and almost dropped her plate. This was a Matt Caldwell she'd never seen before. His usual smile and easygoing attitude were conspicuous for their absence tonight. Boles must really have upset him!

Matt sat down on the other side of Leslie, his eyes darkening as he saw the life abruptly drain out of her. Her body tensed. Her fingers on her plate went white.

"Here, Carolyn, trade places with me," Matt said suddenly, and with a forced smile. "This chair's too low for me."

"I don't think mine's much higher, darling, but I'll do it," Carolyn said in a docile tone.

Leslie relaxed. She smiled shyly at the other woman and then turned her attention back to the woman on the stage.

"Isn't she marvelous?" Carolyn asked. "She's from the Yucatán."

"Not only talented, but pretty as well," Ed agreed. "I love that beat."

"Oh, so do I," Leslie said breathlessly, nibbling a finger sandwich but with her whole attention on the band and the singer.

Matt found himself watching her, amused and touched by her uninhibited joy in the music. It had occurred to him that not much affected her in the office. Here, she was unsure of herself and nervous. Perhaps she even felt out of place. But when the band was playing and the vocalist was singing, she was a different person. He got a glimpse of the way she had been, perhaps, before whatever blows of fate had made her so uneasy around him. He was intrigued by her, and not solely because she wounded his ego. She was a complex person.

Ed noticed Matt's steady gaze on Leslie, and he wanted to drag his cousin aside and tell him the whole miserable story. Matt was curious about Leslie, and he was a bulldozer when he wanted something. He'd run roughshod right over her to get his answers, and Leslie would retreat into the shell her experiences had built around her. She was just coming into the sunlight, and here was Matt driving her back into shadow. Why couldn't Matt be content with Carolyn's adoration? Most women flocked around him; Leslie didn't. He was sure that was the main attraction she held for his cousin. But Matt, pursuing her interest, could set her back years. He had no idea what sort of damage he could do to her fragile emotions.

The singer finished her song, and the audience applauded. She introduced the members of the band and the next number, a beautiful, rhythmic feast called "Brazil." It was Leslie's very favorite piece of music, and she could dance to it, despite her leg. She longed, ached, for someone to take her on the dance floor and let her show those stiff, inhibited people how to fly to that poignant rhythm!

Watching her, Matt saw the hunger in her eyes. Ed couldn't do those steps, but he could. Without a word, he handed Carolyn his empty plate and got to his feet.

Before Leslie had a chance to hesitate or refuse outright, he pulled her gently out of her seat and onto the dance floor.

His dark eyes met her shocked pale ones as he

caught her waist in one lean, strong hand and took her left hand quite reverently into his right one.

"I won't make any sudden turns," he assured her. He nodded once, curtly, to mark the rhythm.

And then he did something remarkable.

Leslie caught her breath as she recognized his ability. She forgot to be afraid of him. She forgot that she was nervous to be held by a man. She was caught up in the rhythm and the delight of having a partner who knew how to dance to perfection the intricate steps that accompanied the Latin beat.

"You're good," Matt mused, smiling with genuine pleasure as they measured their quick steps to the rhythm.

"So are you." She smiled back.

"If your leg gives you trouble, let me know and I'll get you off the floor. Okay?"

"Okay."

"Then let's go!"

He moved her across the floor with the skill of a professional dancer and she followed him with such perfection that other dancers stopped and got out of the way, moving to the sidelines to watch what had become pure entertainment.

Matt and Leslie, enjoying the music and their own interpretation of it, were blind to the other guests, to the smiling members of the band, to everything except the glittering excitement of the dance. They moved as if they were bound by invisible strings, each to the other, with perfectly matching steps.

As the music finally wound down, Matt drew her in close against his lean frame and tilted her down in an elegant, but painful, finish.

The applause was thunderous. Matt drew Leslie upright again and noticed how pale and drawn her face was.

"Too much too soon," he murmured. "Come on. Off you go."

He didn't move closer. Instead, he held out his arm and let her come to him, let her catch hold of it where the muscle was thickest. She clung with both hands, hating herself for doing something so incredibly stupid. But, oh, it had been fun! It was worth the pain.

She didn't realize she'd spoken aloud until Matt eased her down into her chair again.

"Do you have any aspirin in that tiny thing?" Matt asked, indicating the small string purse on her arm.

She grimaced.

"Of course not." He turned, scanning the audience. "Back in a jiffy."

He moved off in the general direction of the punch bowl while Ed caught Leslie's hand in his. "That was great," he enthused. "Just great! I didn't know you could dance like that."

"Neither did I," she murmured shyly.

"Quite an exhibition," Carolyn agreed coolly. "But silly to do something so obviously painful. Now Matt will spend the rest of the night blaming himself and trying to find aspirin, I suppose." She got up and marched off with her barely touched plate and Matt's empty one.

"Well, she's in a snit," Ed observed. "She can't dance like that."

"I shouldn't have done it," Leslie murmured. "But it was so much fun, Ed! I felt alive, really alive!"

"You looked it. Nice to see your eyes light up again."

She made a face at him. "I've spoiled Carolyn's evening."

"Fair trade," he murmured dryly, "she spoiled mine the minute she got into the limousine and complained that I smelled like a sweets shop."

"You smell very nice," she replied.

He smiled. "Thanks."

Matt was suddenly coming back toward them, with Lou Coltrain by the arm. It looked as if she were being forcibly escorted across the floor and Ed had to hide the grin he couldn't help.

"Well," Lou huffed, staring at Matt before she lowered her gaze to Leslie. "I thought you were dying, considering the way he appropriated me and dragged me over here!"

"I don't have any aspirin," Leslie said uneasily. "I'm sorry…"

"There's nothing to be sorry about," Lou said instantly. She patted Leslie's hand gently. "But you've had some pretty bad bruising and this isn't the sort of exercise I'd recommend. Shattered bones are never as strong, even when they're set properly—and yours were not.''

Embarrassed, Leslie bit her lower lip.

''You'll be okay,'' Lou promised with a gentle smile. ''In fact, exercise is good for the muscles that support that bone—it makes it stronger. But don't do this again for a couple of weeks, at least. Here. I always carry aspirin!''

She handed Leslie a small metal container of aspirin and Matt produced another cup of soda water and stood over her, unsmiling, while she took two of the aspirins and swallowed them.

''Thanks,'' she told Lou. ''I really appreciate it.''

''You come and see me Monday,'' Lou instructed, her dark eyes full of authority. ''I'll write you a prescription for something that will make your life easier. Not narcotics,'' she added with a smile. ''Antiinflammatories. They'll make a big difference in the way you get around.''

''You're a nice doctor,'' she told Lou solemnly.

Lou's eyes narrowed. ''I gather that you've known some who weren't.''

''One, at least,'' she said in a cold tone. She smiled at Lou. ''You've changed my mind about doctors.''

''That's one point for me. I'll rush right over and tell Copper,'' she added, smiling as she caught her redheaded husband's eyes across the room. ''He'll be impressed!''

''Not much impresses the other Doctor Coltrain,''

Matt told her after Lou was out of earshot. "Lou did."

"Not until he knew she had a whole closetful of Lionel electric trains," Ed commented with a chuckle.

"Their son has a lot to look forward to when he grows up," Matt mused. He glanced beside Leslie. "Where's Carolyn?"

"She left in a huff," Ed said.

"I'll go find her. Sure you'll be okay?" he asked Leslie with quiet concern.

She nodded. "Thanks for the aspirin. They really help."

He nodded. His dark eyes slid over her drawn face and then away as he went in search of his date.

"I've spoiled his evening, too, I guess," she said wistfully.

"You can't take credit for that," Ed told her. "I've hardly ever seen Matt having so much fun as he was when he was dancing with you. Most of the women around here can only do a two-step. You're a miracle on the dance floor."

"I love to dance," she sighed. "I always did. Mama was so light on her feet." Her eyes twinkled with fond memories. "I used to love to watch her when I was little and she danced with Daddy. She was so pretty, so full of life." The light went out of her eyes. "She thought I'd encouraged Mike, and the others, too," she said dully. "She…shot him and the bullet went through him, into my leg…"

''So that's how your leg got in that shape.''

She glanced at him, hardly aware of what she'd been saying. She nodded. ''The doctor in the emergency room was sure it was all my fault. That's why my leg wasn't properly set. He removed the bullet and not much else. It wasn't until afterward that another doctor put a cast on. Later, I began to limp. But there was no money for any other doctor visits by then. Mama was in jail and I was all alone. If it hadn't been for my best friend Jessica's family, I wouldn't even have had a home. They took me in despite the gossip and I got to finish school.''

''I'll never know how you managed that,'' Ed said. ''Going to school every day with the trial making headlines week by week.''

''It was tough,'' she agreed. ''But it made me tough, too. Fire tempers steel, don't they say? I'm tempered.''

''Yes, you are.''

She smiled at him. ''Thanks for bringing me. It was wonderful.''

''Tell Matt that. It might change him.''

''Oh, he's not so bad, I think,'' she replied. ''He dances like an angel.''

He stared toward the punch bowl, where Matt was glancing toward him and Leslie. The dark face was harder than stone and Ed felt a tingle of apprehension when Matt left Carolyn and started walking toward them. He didn't like that easygoing stride of Matt's. The only time Matt moved that slowly was when he was homicidally angry.

Chapter Four

Leslie knew by the look in Matt's eyes that he was furious. She thought his anger must be directed toward her, although she couldn't remember anything she'd done to deserve it. As he approached them, he had his cellular phone out and was pushing a number into it. He said something, then closed it and put it back in his pocket.

"I'm sorry, but we have to leave," he said, every syllable dripping ice. "It seems that Carolyn has developed a vicious headache."

"It's all right," Leslie said, and even smiled as relief swept over her that she hadn't put that expression on his handsome face. "I wouldn't have been able to dance again." Her eyes met Matt's shyly. "I really enjoyed it."

He didn't reply. His eyes were narrow and not very friendly. "Ed, will you go out front and watch for the car? I've just phoned the driver."

"Sure." He hesitated noticeably for a moment before he left.

Matt stood looking down at Leslie with an intensity that made her uncomfortable. "You make yourself out to be a broken stick," he said quietly. "But you're not what you appear to be, are you? I get the feeling that you used to be quite a dancer before that leg slowed you down."

She was puzzled. "I learned how from my mother," she said honestly. "I used to dance with her."

He laughed curtly. "Pull the other one," he said. He was thinking about her pretended revulsion, the way she constantly backed off when he came near her. Then, tonight, the carefully planned capitulation. It was an old trick that had been used on him before—backing away so that he'd give chase. He was surprised that he hadn't realized it sooner. He wondered how far she'd let him go. He was going to find out.

She blinked and frowned. "I beg your pardon?" she asked, genuinely puzzled.

"Never mind," he said with a parody of a smile. "Ed should be outside with the driver by now. Shall we go?"

He reached out a lean hand and pulled her to her feet abruptly. Her face was very pale at the hint of domination not only in his eyes, but the hold he had on her. It was hard not to panic. It reminded her of another man who had used domination; only that time she had no knowledge of how to get away. Now she did. She turned her arm quickly and pushed it down against his thumb, the weakest spot in his hold, freeing herself instantly as the self-defense instructor had taught her.

Matt was surprised. "Where did you learn that? From your mother?" he drawled.

"No. From my Tae Kwon Do instructor in Houston," she returned. "Despite my bad leg, I can take care of myself."

"Oh, I'd bet on that." His dark eyes narrowed and glittered faintly. "You're not what you seem, Miss Murry. I'm going to make it my business to find out the truth about you."

She blanched. She didn't want him digging into her past. She'd run from it, hidden from it, for years. Would she have to run some more, just when she felt secure?

He saw her frightened expression and felt even more certain that he'd almost been taken for the ride of his life. Hadn't his experience with women taught him how to recognize deceit? He thought of his mother and his heart went cold. Leslie even had a look of her, with that blond hair. He took her by the upper arm and pulled her along with him, noticing that she moved uncomfortably and tugged at his hold.

"Please," she said tightly. "Slow down. It hurts."

He stopped at once, realizing that he was forcing her to a pace that made walking painful. He'd forgotten about her disability, as if it were part of her act. He let out an angry breath.

"The damaged leg is real," he said, almost to himself. "But what else is?"

She met his angry eyes. "Mr. Caldwell, whatever I am, I'm no threat to you," she said quietly. "I really don't like being touched, but I enjoyed dancing with you. I haven't danced...in years."

He studied her wan face, oblivious to the music of the band, and the murmur of movement around them. "Sometimes," he murmured, "you seem very familiar to me, as if I've seen you before." He was thinking about his mother, and how she'd betrayed him and hurt him all those years ago.

Leslie didn't know that, though. Her teeth clenched as she tried not to let her fear show. Probably he had seen her before, just like the whole country had, her face in the tabloid papers as it had appeared the night they took her out of her mother's bloodstained apartment on a stretcher, her leg bleeding profusely, her sobs audible. But then her hair had been dark, and she'd been wearing glasses. Could he really recognize her?

"Maybe I just have that kind of face." She grimaced and shifted her weight. "Could we go, please?" she asked on a moan. "My leg really is killing me."

He didn't move for an instant. Then he bent suddenly and lifted her in his strong arms and carried her through the amused crowd toward the door.

"Mr....Mr. Caldwell," she protested, stiffening. She'd never been picked up and carried by a man in her entire life. She studied his strong profile with fascinated curiosity, too entranced to feel the usual fear. Having danced with him, she was able to accept his physical closeness. He felt very strong and he smelled of some spicy, very exotic cologne. She had the oddest urge to touch his wavy black hair just over his broad forehead, where it looked thickest.

He glanced down into her fascinated eyes and one of his dark eyebrows rose in a silent question.

"You're...very strong, aren't you?" she asked hesitantly.

The tone of her voice touched something deep inside him. He searched her eyes and the tension was suddenly thick as his gaze fell to her soft bow of a mouth and lingered there, even as his pace slowed slightly.

Her hand clutched the lapel of his tuxedo as her own gaze fell to his mouth. She'd never wanted to be kissed like this before. When she'd been kissed during that horrible encounter, it had been repulsive—a wet, invading, lustful kiss that made her want to throw up.

It wouldn't be like that with Matt. She knew instinctively that he was well versed in the art of love-making, and that he would be gentle with a woman.

His mouth was sensual, wide and chiseled. Her own mouth tingled as she wondered visibly what it would feel like to let him kiss her.

He read that curiosity with pinpoint accuracy and his sharp intake of breath brought her curious eyes up to meet his.

"Careful," he cautioned, his voice deeper than usual. "Curiosity killed the cat."

Her eyes asked a question she couldn't form with her lips.

"You fell off a horse avoiding any contact with me," he reminded her quietly. "Now you look as if you'd do anything to have my mouth on yours. Why?"

"I don't know," she whispered, her hand contracting on the lapel of his jacket. "I like being close to you," she confessed, surprised. "It's funny. I haven't wanted to be close to a man like this before."

He stopped dead in his tracks. There was a faint vibration in the hard arms holding her. His eyes lanced into hers. His breath became audible. The arm under her back contracted, bringing her breasts hard against him as he stood there on the steps of the building, totally oblivious to everything except the ache that was consuming him.

Leslie's body shivered with its first real taste of desire. She laughed shakily at the new and wonderful sensations she was feeling. Her breasts felt suddenly heavy. They ached.

"Is this what it feels like?" she murmured.

"What?" he asked huskily.

She met his gaze. "Desire."

He actually shuddered. His arms contracted. His lips parted as he looked at her mouth and knew that he couldn't help taking it. She smelled of roses, like the tiny pink fairy roses that grew in masses around the front door of his ranch house. She wanted him. His head began to spin. He bent his dark head and bit at her lower lip with a sensuous whisper.

"Open your mouth, Leslie," he whispered, and his hard mouth suddenly went down insistently on hers.

But before he could even savor the feel of her soft lips, the sound of high heels approaching jerked his head up. Leslie was trembling against him, shocked and a little frightened, and completely entranced by the unexpected contact with his beautiful mouth.

Matt's dark eyes blazed down into hers. "No more games. I'm taking you home with me," he said huskily.

She started to speak, to protest, when Carolyn came striding angrily out the door.

"Does she have to be carried?" the older woman asked Matt with dripping sarcasm. "Funny, she was dancing eagerly enough a few minutes ago!"

"She has a bad leg," Matt said, regaining his control. "Here's the car."

The limousine drew up at the curb and Ed got out, frowning when he saw Leslie in Matt's arms.

"Are you all right?" he asked as he approached them.

"She shouldn't have danced," Matt said stiffly as he moved the rest of the way down the steps to deposit her inside the car on the leather-covered seat. "She made her leg worse."

Carolyn was livid. She slid in and moved to the other side of Leslie with a gaze that could have curdled milk. "One dance and we have to leave," she said furiously.

Matt moved into the car beside Ed and slammed the door. "I thought we were leaving because you had a headache," he snapped at Carolyn, his usual control quite evidently gone. He was in a foul mood. Desire was frustrating him. He glanced at Leslie and thought how good she was at manipulation. She had him almost doubled over with need. She was probably laughing her head off silently. Well, she was going to pay for that.

Carolyn, watching his eyes on Leslie, made an angry sound in her throat and stared out the window.

To Ed's surprise and dismay, they dropped him off at his home first. He tried to argue, but Matt wasn't having that. He told Ed he'd see him at the office Monday and closed the door on his protests.

Carolyn was deposited next. Matt walked her to her door, but he moved back before she could claim a good-night kiss. The way she slammed her door was audible even inside the closed limousine.

Leslie bit her lower lip as Matt climbed back into the car with her. In the lighted interior, she could see the expression on his face as he studied her slender body covetously.

"This isn't the way to my apartment," she ventured nervously a few minutes later, hoping he hadn't meant what he said just before they got into the limousine.

"No, it isn't, is it?" he replied dangerously.

Even as he spoke, the limousine pulled up at the door to his ranch house. He helped Leslie out and spoke briefly to the driver before dismissing him. Then he swung a frightened Leslie up into his arms and carried her toward the front door.

"Mr. Caldwell…" she began.

"Matt," he corrected, not looking at her.

"I want to go home," she tried again.

"You will. Eventually."

"But you sent the car away."

"I have six cars," he informed her as he shifted his light burden to produce his keys from the pocket of his slacks and insert one in the lock. The door swung open. "I'll drive you home when the time comes."

"I'm very tired." Her voice sounded breathless and high-pitched.

"Then I know just the place for you." He closed the door and carried her down a long, dimly lit hallway to a room near the back of the house. He leaned down to open the door and once they were through it, he kicked it shut with his foot.

Seconds later, Leslie was in the middle of a huge

king-size bed, sprawled on the beige-brown-and-black comforter that covered it and Matt was removing her wrap.

It went flying onto a chair, along with his jacket and tie. He unbuttoned his shirt and slid down onto the bed beside her, his hands on either side of her face as he poised just above her.

The position brought back terrible, nightmarish memories. She stiffened all over. Her face went pale. Her eyes dilated so much that the gray of them was eclipsed by black.

Matt ignored her expression. He looked down the length of her in the clinging silver dress, his eyes lingering on the thrust of her small breasts. One of his big hands came up to trace around the prominent hard nipple that pointed through the fabric.

The touch shocked Leslie, because she didn't find it revolting or unpleasant. She shivered a little. Her eyes, wide and frightened, and a little curious, met his.

His strong fingers brushed lazily over the nipple and around the contours of her breast as if the feel of her fascinated him.

"Do you mind?" he asked with faint insolence, and slipped one of the spaghetti straps down her arm, moving her just enough that he could pull the bodice away from her perfect little breast.

Leslie couldn't believe what was happening. Men were repulsive to her. She hated the thought of intimacy. But Matt Caldwell was looking at her bare breast and she was letting him, with no thought of resistance. She hadn't even had anything to drink.

He searched her face as his warm fingers traced her breast. He read the pleasure she was feeling in her soft eyes. "You feel like sun-touched marble to my hand," he said quietly. "Your skin is beautiful." His gaze traveled down her body. "Your breasts are perfect."

She was shivering again. Her hands clenched beside her head as she watched him touch her, like an observer, like in a dream.

He smiled with faint mockery when he saw her expression. "Haven't you done this before?"

"No," she said, and she actually sounded serious.

He discounted that at once. She was far too calm and submissive for an inexperienced woman.

One dark eyebrow lifted. "Twenty-three and still a virgin?"

How had he known that? "Well...yes." Technically she certainly was. Emotionally, too. Despite what had been done to her, she'd been spared rape, if only by seconds, when her mother came home unexpectedly.

Matt was absorbed in touching her body. His forefinger traced around the hard nipple, and he watched her body lift to follow it when he lifted his hand.

"Do you like it?" he asked softly.

She was watching him intensely. "Yes." She sounded as if it surprised her that she liked what he was doing.

With easy self-confidence, he pulled her up just a little and pushed the other strap down her arm, baring her completely to his eyes. She was perfect, like a warm statue in beautifully smooth marble. He'd never seen breasts like hers. She aroused him profoundly.

He held her by the upper part of her rib cage, his thumbs edging onto her breasts to caress them tenderly while he watched the expressions chase each other across her face. The silence in the bedroom was broken only by the sound of cars far in the distance and the sound of some mournful night bird outside the window. Closer was the rasp of her own breathing and her heart beating in her ears. She should be fighting for her life, screaming, running, escaping. She'd avoided this sort of situation successfully for six years. Why didn't she want to avoid Matt's hands?

Matt touched her almost reverently, his eyes on her hard nipples. With a faint groan, he bent his dark head and his mouth touched the soft curve of her breast.

She gasped and stiffened. His head lifted immediately. He looked at her and realized that she wasn't trying to get away. Her eyes were full of shocked pleasure and curiosity.

"Another first?" he asked with faint arrogance and a calculating smile that didn't really register in her whirling mind.

She nodded, swallowing. Her body, as if it was

ignoring her brain, moved sensuously on the bed. She'd never dreamed that she could let a man touch her like this, that she could enjoy letting him touch her, after her one horrible experience with intimacy.

He put his mouth over her nipple and suckled her so insistently that she cried out, drowning in a veritable flood of shocked pleasure.

The little cry aroused Matt unexpectedly, and he was rougher with her than he meant to be, his mouth suddenly demanding on her soft flesh. He tasted her hungrily for several long seconds until he forced his mind to remember why he shouldn't let himself go in headfirst. He wanted her almost beyond bearing, but he wasn't going to let her make a fool of him.

He lifted his head and studied her flushed face clinically. She was enjoying it, but she needn't think he was going to let her take possession of him with that pretty body. He knew now that he could have her. She was willing to give in. For a price, he added.

She opened her eyes and lay there watching him with wide, soft, curious eyes. She thought she had him in her pocket, he mused. But she was all too acquiescent. That, he thought amusedly, was a gross miscalculation on her part. It was her nervous retreat that challenged him, not the sort of easy conquest with which he was already too familiar.

Abruptly he sat up, pulling her with him, and slid the straps of her evening dress back up onto her shoulders.

She watched him silently, still shocked by his ardor and puzzled at her unexpected response to it.

He got to his feet and rebuttoned his shirt, reaching for his snap-on tie and then his jacket. He studied her there, sitting dazed on the edge of his bed, and his dark eyes narrowed. He smiled, but it wasn't a pleasant smile.

"You're not bad," he murmured lazily. "But the fascinated virgin bit turns me right off. I like experience."

She blinked. She was still trying to make her mind work again.

"I assume that your other would-be lovers liked that wide-eyed, first-time look?"

Other lovers. Had he guessed about her past? Her eyes registered the fear.

He saw it. He was vaguely sorry that she wasn't what she pretended to be. He was all but jaded when it came to pursuing women. He hated the coy behavior, the teasing, the manipulation that eventually ended in his bedroom. He was considered a great catch by single women, rich and handsome and experienced in sensual techniques. But he always made his position clear at the outset. He didn't want marriage. That didn't really matter to most of the women in his life. A diamond here, an exotic vacation there, and they seemed satisfied for as long as it lasted. Not that there were many affairs. He was tired of the game. In fact, he'd never been more tired of it than he was right now. His whole expression was one of disgust.

Leslie saw it in his eyes and wished she could curl up into a ball and hide under the bed. His cold scrutiny made her feel cheap, just as that doctor had, just as the media had, just as her mother had…

He couldn't have explained why that expression on her face made him feel guilty. But it did.

He turned away from her. "Come on," he said, picking up her wrap and purse and tossing them to her. "I'll run you home."

She didn't look at him as she followed him down the length of the hall. It was longer than she realized, and even before they got to the front door, her leg was throbbing. Dancing had been damaging enough, without the jerk of his hand as they left the ballroom. But she ground her teeth together and didn't let her growing discomfort show in her face. He wasn't going to make her feel any worse than she already did by accusing her of putting on an act for sympathy. She went past him out the door he was holding open, avoiding his eyes. She wondered how things could have gone so terribly wrong.

The spacious garage was full of cars. He got out the silver Mercedes and opened the door to let her climb inside, onto the leather-covered passenger seat. He closed her door with something of a snap. Her fingers fumbled the seat belt into its catch and she hoped he wouldn't want to elaborate on what he'd already said.

She stared out the window at the dark silhouettes of buildings and trees as he drove along the back roads that eventually led into Jacobsville. She was sick about the way she'd acted. He probably thought she was the easiest woman alive. The only thing she didn't understand was why he didn't take advantage of it. The obvious reason made her even more uncomfortable. Didn't they say that some men didn't want what came easily? It was probably true. He'd been in pursuit as long as she was backing away from him. What irony, to spend years being afraid of men, running crazily from even the most platonic involvement, to find herself capable of torrid desire with the one man in the world who didn't want her!

He felt her tension. It was all too apparent that she was disappointed that he hadn't played the game to its finish.

"Is that what Ed gets when he takes you home?" he drawled.

Her nails bit into her small evening bag. Her teeth clenched. She wasn't going to dignify that remark with a reply.

He shrugged and paused to turn onto the main highway. "Don't take it so hard," he said lazily. "I'm a little too sophisticated to fall for it, but there are a few rich single ranchers around Jacobsville. Cy Parks comes to mind. He's hell on the nerves, but he is a widower." He glanced at her averted face. "On second thought, he's had enough tragedy in his life. I wouldn't wish you on him.''

She couldn't even manage to speak, she was so choked up with hurt. Why, she wondered, did everything she wanted in life turn on her and tear her to pieces? It was like tracking cougars with a toy gun. Just when she seemed to find peace and purpose, her life became nothing but torment. As if her tattered pride wasn't enough, she was in terrible pain. She shifted in the seat, hoping that a change of position would help. It didn't.

''How did that bone get shattered?'' he asked conversationally.

''Don't you know?'' she asked on a harsh laugh. If he'd seen the story about her, as she suspected, he was only playing a cruel game—the sort of game he'd already accused her of playing!

He glanced at her with a scowl. ''And how would I know?'' he wondered aloud.

She frowned. Maybe he hadn't read anything at all! He might be fishing for answers.

She swallowed, gripping her purse tightly.

He swung the Mercedes into the driveway of her boardinghouse and pulled up at the steps, with the engine still running. He turned to her. ''How *would* I know?'' he asked again, his voice determined.

''You seem to think you're an expert on everything else about me,'' she replied evasively.

His chin lifted as he studied her through narrowed

eyes. "There are several ways a bone can be shattered," he said quietly. "One way is from a bullet."

She didn't feel as if she were still breathing. She sat like a statue, watching him deliberate.

"What do you know about bullets?" she asked shortly.

"My unit was called up during Operation Desert Storm," he told her. "I served with an infantry unit. I know quite a lot about bullets. And what they do to bone," he added. "Which brings me to the obvious question. Who shot you?"

"I didn't say...I was shot," she managed.

His intense gaze held her like invisible ropes. "But you were, weren't you?" he asked with shrewd scrutiny. His lips tugged into a cold smile. "As to who did it, I'd bet on one of your former lovers. Did he catch you with somebody else, or did you tease him the way you teased me tonight and then refuse him?" He gave her another contemptuous look. "Not that you refused. You didn't exactly play hard to get."

Her ego went right down to her shoes. He was painting her over with evil colors. She bit her lower lip. It was unpleasant enough to have her memories, but to have this man making her out to be some sort of nymphomaniac was painful beyond words. Her first real taste of tender intimacy had been with him, tonight, and he made it sound dirty and cheap.

She unfastened her seat belt and got out of the car with as much dignity as she could muster. Her leg was incredibly painful. All she wanted was her bed, her heating pad and some more aspirins. And to get away from her tormenter.

Matt switched off the engine and moved around the car, irritated by the way she limped.

"I'll take you to the door...!"

She flinched when he came close. She backed away from him, actually shivering when she remembered shamefully what she'd let him do to her. Her eyes clouded with unshed angry tears, with outraged virtue.

"More games?" he asked tersely. He hadn't liked having her back away again after the way she'd been in his bedroom.

"I don't...play games," she replied, hating the hiccup of a sob that revealed how upset she really was. She clutched her wrap and her purse to her chest, accusing eyes glaring at him. "And you can go to hell!"

He scowled at the way she looked, barely hearing the words. She was white in the face and her whole body seemed rigid, as if she really was upset.

She turned and walked away, wincing inwardly with every excruciating step, to the front porch. But her face didn't show one trace of her discomfort. She held her head high. She still had her pride, she thought through a wave of pain.

Matt watched her go into the boardinghouse with more mixed, confused emotions than he'd ever felt.

He remembered vividly that curious "Don't you know?" when he'd asked who shot her.

He got back into the Mercedes and sat staring through the windshield for a long moment before he started it. Miss Murry was one puzzle he intended to solve, and if it cost him a fortune in detective fees, he was going to do it.

Chapter Five

Leslie cried for what seemed hours. The aspirin didn't help the leg pain at all. There was no medicine known to man that she could take for her wounded ego. Matt had swept the floor with her, played with her, laughed at her naiveté and made her out to be little better than a prostitute. He was like that emergency room doctor so long ago who'd made her ashamed of her body. It was a pity that her first real desire for a man's touch had made her an object of contempt to the man himself.

Well, she told herself as she wiped angrily at the tears, she'd never make that mistake again. Matt Caldwell could go right where she'd told him to!

The phone rang and she hesitated to answer it. But it might be Ed. She picked up the receiver.

"We had a good laugh about you," Carolyn told her outright. "I guess you'll think twice before you throw yourself at him again! He said you were so easy that you disgusted him…!"

Almost shaking with humiliation, she put the receiver down with a slam and then unplugged the phone. It was so close to what Matt had already said that there was no reason not to believe her. Carolyn's harsh arrogance was just what she needed to make the miserable evening complete.

The pain, combined with the humiliation, kept her awake until almost daylight. She missed breakfast, not to mention church, and when she did finally open her eyes, it was to a kind of pain she hadn't experienced since the night she was shot.

She shifted, wincing, and then moaned as the movement caused another searing wave of discomfort up her leg. The knock on her door barely got through to her. "Come in," she said in a husky, exhausted tone.

The door opened and there was Matt Caldwell, unshaven and with dark circles under his eyes.

Carolyn's words came back to haunt her. She grabbed the first thing that came to hand, a plastic bottle of spring water she kept by the bed, and flung it furiously across the room at him. It missed his head, and Ed's, by a quarter of an inch.

"No, thanks," Ed said, moving in front of Matt. "I don't want any water."

Her face was lined with pain, white with it. She glared at Matt's hard, angry face with eyes that would have looked perfectly natural over a cocked pistol.

"I couldn't get you on the phone, and I was worried," Ed said gently, approaching her side of the double bed she occupied. He noticed the unplugged telephone on her bedside table. "Now I know why I couldn't get you on the phone." He studied her drawn face. "How bad is it?"

She could barely breathe. "Bad," she said huskily, thinking what an understatement that word was.

He took her thick white chenille bathrobe from the chair beside the bed. "Come on. We're going to drive you to the emergency room. Matt can phone Lou Coltrain and have her meet us there."

It was an indication of the pain that she didn't argue. She got out of bed, aware of the picture she must make in the thick flannel pajamas that covered every inch of her up to her chin. Matt was probably shocked, she thought as she let Ed stuff her into the robe. He probably expected her to be naked under the covers, conforming to the image he had of her nymphomania!

He hadn't said a word. He just stood there, by the door, grimly watching Ed get her ready—until she tried to walk, and folded up.

Ed swung her up in his arms, stopping Matt's instinctive quick movement toward her. Ed knew for a fact that she'd scream the house down if his cousin so much as touched her. He didn't know what had gone on the night before, but judging by the way Matt and Leslie looked, it had been both humiliating and embarrassing.

"I can carry her," he told Matt. "Let's go."

Matt glimpsed her contorted features and didn't hesitate. He led the way down the hall and right out the front door.

"My purse," she said huskily. "My insurance card…"

"That can be taken care of later," Matt said stiffly. He opened the back door of the Mercedes and waited while Ed slid her onto the seat.

She leaned back with her eyes closed, almost sick from the pain.

"She should never have gotten on the dance floor," Matt said through his teeth as they started toward town. "And then I jerked her up out of her chair. It's my fault."

Ed didn't reply. He glanced over the seat at Leslie with concern in his whole expression. He hoped she hadn't done any major damage to herself with that exhibition the night before.

Lou Coltrain was waiting in the emergency room as Ed carried Leslie inside the building. She motioned him down the hall to a room and closed the door behind Matt as soon as he entered.

She examined the leg carefully, asking questions that Leslie was barely able to answer. "I want

X rays,'' she said. ''But I'll give you something for pain first.''

''Thank you,'' Leslie choked, fighting tears.

Lou smoothed her wild hair. ''You poor little thing,'' she said softly. ''Cry if you want to. It must hurt like hell.''

She went out to get the injection, and tears poured down Leslie's face because of that tender concern. She hardly ever cried. She was tough. She could take anything—near-rape, bullet wounds, notoriety, her mother's trial, the refusal of her parent to even speak to her...

''There, there,'' Ed said. He produced a handkerchief and blotted the tears, smiling down at her. ''Dr. Lou is going to make it all better.''

''For God's sake...!'' Matt bit off angry words and walked out of the room. It was unbearable that he'd hurt her like that. Unbearable! And then to have to watch Ed comforting her...!

''I hate him,'' Leslie choked when he was gone. She actually shivered. ''He laughed about it,'' she whispered, blind to Ed's curious scowl. ''She said they both laughed about it, that he was disgusted.''

''She?''

''Carolyn.'' The tears were hot in her eyes, cold on her cheeks. ''I hate him!''

Lou came back with the injection and gave it, waiting for it to take effect. She glanced at Ed. ''You might want to wait outside. I'm taking her down to

X ray myself. I'll come and get you when we've done some tests.''

"Okay.''

He went out and joined Matt in the waiting room. The older man's face was drawn, tormented. He barely glanced at Ed before he turned his attention to the trees outside the window. It was a dismal gray day, with rain threatening. It matched his mood.

Ed leaned against the wall beside him with a frown. "She said Carolyn phoned her last night,'' he began. "I suppose that's why the phone was unplugged.''

It was Matt's turn to look puzzled. "What?''

"Leslie said Carolyn told her the two of you were laughing at her,'' he murmured. "She didn't say what about.''

Matt's face hardened visibly. He rammed his hands into his pockets and his eyes were terrible to look into.

"Don't hurt Leslie,'' Ed said suddenly, his voice quiet but full of venom. "She hasn't had an easy life. Don't make things hard on her. She has no place else to go.''

Matt glanced at him, disliking the implied threat as much as the fact that Ed knew far more about Leslie than he did. Were they lovers? Old lovers, perhaps?

"She keeps secrets,'' he said. "She was shot. Who did it?''

Ed lifted both eyebrows. "Who said she was

shot?'' he asked innocently, doing it so well that he actually fooled his cousin.

Matt hesitated. ''Nobody. I assumed…well, how else does a bone get shattered?''

''By a blow, by a bad fall, in a car wreck…'' Ed trailed off, leaving Matt with something to think about.

''Yes. Of course.'' The older man sighed. ''Dancing put her in this shape. I didn't realize just how fragile she was. She doesn't exactly shout her problems to the world.''

''She was always like that,'' Ed replied.

Matt turned to face him. ''How did you meet her?''

''She and I were in college together,'' Ed told him. ''We used to date occasionally. She trusts me,'' he added.

Matt was turning what he knew about Leslie over in his mind. If the pieces had been part of a puzzle, none of them would fit. When they first met, she avoided his touch like the plague. Last night, she'd enjoyed his advances. She'd been nervous and shy at their first meeting. Later, at the office, she'd been gregarious, almost playful. Last night, she'd been a completely different woman on the dance floor. Then, when he'd taken her home with him, she'd been hungry, sensuous, tender. Nothing about her made any sense.

''Don't trust her too far,'' Matt advised the other

man. "She's too secretive to suit me. I thinks she's hiding something…maybe something pretty bad."

Ed didn't dare react. He pursed his lips and smiled. "Leslie's never hurt anyone in her life," he remarked. "And before you get the wrong idea about her, you'd better know that she has a real fear of men."

Matt laughed. "Oh, that's a good one," he said mockingly. "You should have seen her last night when we were alone."

Ed's eyes narrowed. "What do you mean?"

"I mean she's easy," Matt said with a contemptuous smile.

Ed's eyes began to glitter. He called his cousin a name that made Matt's eyebrows arch.

"Easy. My God!" Ed ground out.

Matt was puzzled by the other man's inexplicable behavior. Probably he was jealous. His cell phone began to trill, diverting him. He answered it. He recognized Carolyn's voice immediately and moved away, so that Ed couldn't hear what he said. Ed was certainly acting strange lately.

"I thought you were coming over to ride with me this afternoon," Carolyn said cheerfully. "Where are you?"

"At the hospital," he said absently, his eyes on Ed's retreating back going through the emergency room doors. "What did you say to Leslie last night?"

"What do you mean?"

"When you phoned her!" Matt prompted.

Carolyn sounded vague. "Well, I wanted to see if she was better," she replied. "She seemed to be in a lot of pain after the dance."

"What else did you say?"

Carolyn laughed. "Oh, I see. I'm being accused of something underhanded, is that it? Really, Matt, I thought you could see through that phony vulnerability of hers. What did she tell you I said?"

He shrugged. "Never mind. I must have misunderstood."

"You certainly did," she assured him firmly. "I wouldn't call someone in pain to upset them. I thought you knew me better than that."

"I do." He was seething. So now it seemed that Miss Murry was making up lies about Carolyn. Had it been to get even with him, for not giving in to her wiles? Or was she trying to turn his cousin against him?

"What about that horseback ride? And what are you doing at the hospital?" she added suddenly.

"I'm with Ed, visiting one of his friends," he said. "Better put the horseback ride off until next weekend. I'll phone you."

He hung up. His eyes darkened with anger. He wanted the Murry woman out of his company, out of his life. She was going to be nothing but trouble.

He repocketed the phone and went outside to wait for Ed and Leslie.

* * *

A good half hour later, Ed came out of the emergency room with his hands in his pockets, looking worried.

"They're keeping her overnight," he said curtly.

"For a sore leg?" Matt asked with mild sarcasm.

Ed scowled. "One of the bones shifted and it's pressing on a nerve," he replied. "Lou says it won't get any better until it's fixed. They're sending for an orthopedic man from Houston. He'll be in this afternoon."

"Who's going to pay for that?" Matt asked coldly.

"Since you ask, I am," Ed returned, not intimidated even by those glittery eyes.

"It's your money," the older man replied. He let out a breath. "What caused the bone to separate?"

"Why ask a question when you already know the answer?" Ed wanted to know. "I'm going to stay with her. She's frightened."

He was fairly certain that even if Leslie could fake pain, she couldn't fake an X ray. Somewhere in the back of his mind he found guilt lurking. If he hadn't pulled her onto the dance floor, and if he hadn't jerked her to her feet...

He turned away and walked out of the building without another word. Leslie was Ed's business. He kept telling himself that. But all the way home, his conscience stabbed at him. She couldn't help being what she was. Even so, he hadn't meant to hurt her. He remembered the tears, genuine tears, boiling out of her eyes when Lou had touched her hair so gently. She acted as if she'd never had tenderness in her life.

He drove himself home and tried to concentrate on briefing himself for a director's meeting the next day. But long before bedtime, he gave it up and drank himself into uneasy sleep.

The orthopedic man examined the X rays and seconded Lou's opinion that immediate surgery was required. But Leslie didn't want the surgery. She refused to talk about it. The minute the doctors and Ed left the room, she struggled out of bed and hobbled to the closet to pull her pajamas and robe and shoes out of it.

In the hall, Matt came upon Ed and Lou and a tall, distinguished stranger in an expensive suit.

"You two look like stormy weather," he mused. "What's wrong?"

"Leslie won't have the operation," Ed muttered worriedly. "Dr. Santos flew all the way from Houston to do the surgery, and she won't hear of it."

"Maybe she doesn't think she needs it," Matt said.

Lou glanced at him. "You have no idea what sort of pain she's in," she said, impatient with him. "One of the bone fragments, the one that shifted, is pressing right on a nerve."

"The bones should have been properly aligned at the time the accident occurred," the visiting orthopedic surgeon agreed. "It was criminally irresponsible of the attending physician to do nothing more than bandage the leg. A cast wasn't even used until afterward!''

That sounded negligent to Matt, too. He frowned. ''Did she say why not?''

Lou sighed angrily. ''She won't talk about it. She won't listen to any of us. Eventually she'll have to. But in the meantime, the pain is going to drive her insane.''

Matt glanced from one set face to the other and walked past them to Leslie's room.

She was wearing her flannel pajamas and reaching for the robe when Matt walked in. She gave him a glare hot enough to boil water.

''Well, at least you won't be trying to talk me into an operation I don't want,'' she muttered as she struggled to get from the closet to the bed.

''Why won't I?''

She arched both eyebrows expressively. ''I'm the enemy.''

He stood at the foot of the bed, watching her get into the robe. Her leg was at an awkward angle, and her face was pinched. He could imagine the sort of pain she was already experiencing.

''Suit yourself about the operation,'' he replied with forced indifference, folding his arms across his chest. ''But don't expect me to have someone carry you back and forth around the office. If you want to make a martyr of yourself, be my guest.''

She stopped fiddling with the belt of the robe and stared at him quietly, puzzled.

"Some people enjoy making themselves objects of pity to people around them," he continued deliberately.

"I don't want pity!" she snapped.

"Really?"

She wrapped the belt around her fingers and stared at it. "I'll have to be in a cast."

"No doubt."

"My insurance hasn't taken effect yet, either," she said with averted eyes. "Once it's in force, I can have the operation." She looked back at him coldly. "I'm not going to let Ed pay for it, in case you wondered, and I don't care if he can afford it!"

He had to fight back a stirring of admiration for her independent stance. It could be part of the pose, he realized, but it sounded pretty genuine. His blue eyes narrowed. "I'll pay for it," he said, surprising both of them. "It can come out of your weekly check."

Her teeth clenched. "I know how much this sort of thing costs. That's why I've never had it done before. I'd never be able to pay it back in my lifetime."

His eyes fell to her body. "We could work something out," he murmured.

She flushed. "No, we couldn't!"

She stood up, barely able to stand the pain, despite the painkillers they'd given her. She hobbled over to the chair, where her shoes were placed, and eased her feet into them.

"Where are you going?" he asked conversationally.

"Home," she said, and started past him.

He caught her up in his arms like a fallen package and carried her right back to the bed, dumping her on it gently. His arms made a cage as he looked down at her flushed face. "Don't be stupid," he said in a voice that went right through her. "You're no good to yourself or anyone else in this condition. You have no choice."

Her lips trembled as she fought to control the tears. She would be helpless, vulnerable. Besides, that surgeon reminded her of the man at the emergency room in Houston. He brought back unbearable shame.

The unshed tears fascinated Matt. She fascinated him. He didn't want to care about what happened to her, but he did.

He reached down and smoothed a long forefinger over her wet lashes. "Do you have family?" he asked unexpectedly.

She thought of her mother, in prison, and felt sick to her very soul. "No," she whispered starkly.

"Are both your parents dead?"

"Yes," she said at once.

"No brothers, sisters?"

She shook her head.

He frowned, as if her situation disturbed him. In fact, it did. She looked vulnerable and fragile and completely lost. He didn't understand why he cared so much for her well-being. Perhaps it was guilt because he'd lured her into a kind of dancing she wasn't really able to do anymore.

"I want to go home," she said harshly.

"Afterward," he replied.

She remembered him saying that before, in almost the same way, and she averted her face in shame.

He could have bitten his tongue for that. He shouldn't bait her when she was in such a condition. It was hitting below the belt.

He drew in a long breath. "Leave it to Ed to pick up strays, and make me responsible for them!" he muttered, angry because of her vulnerability and his unwanted response to it.

She didn't say a word, but her lower lip trembled and she turned her face away from him. Beside her hip, her hand was clenched so tightly that the knuckles were white.

He shot away from the bed, his eyes furious. "You're having the damned operation," he informed her flatly. "Once you're healthy and whole again, you won't need Ed to prop you up. You can work for your living like every other woman."

She didn't answer him. She didn't look at him. She wanted to get better so that she could kick the hell out of him.

"Did you hear me?" he asked in a dangerously soft tone.

She jerked her head to acknowledge the question but she didn't speak.

He let out an angry breath. "I'll tell the others."

He left her lying there and announced her decision to the three people in the hall.

"How did you manage that?" Ed asked when Lou and Dr. Santos went back in to talk to Leslie.

"I made her mad," Matt replied. "Sympathy doesn't work."

"No, it doesn't," Ed replied quietly. "I don't think she's had much of it in her whole life."

"What happened to her parents?" he wanted to know.

Ed was careful about the reply. "Her father misjudged the position of some electrical wires and flew right into them. He was electrocuted."

He frowned darkly. "And her mother?"

"They were both in love with the same man," Ed said evasively. "He died, and Leslie and her mother still aren't on speaking terms."

Matt turned away, jingling the change in his pocket restlessly. "How did he die?"

"Violently," Ed told him. "It was a long time ago. But I don't think Leslie will ever get over it."

Which was true, but it sounded as if Leslie was still in love with the dead man—which was exactly what Ed wanted. He was going to save her from Matt, whatever it took. She was a good friend. He didn't want her life destroyed because Matt was on the prowl for a new conquest. Leslie deserved something better than to be one of Matt's ex-girlfriends.

Matt glanced at his cousin with a puzzling expression. "When will they operate?"

"Tomorrow morning," Ed said. "I'll be late getting to work. I'm going to be here while it's going on."

Matt nodded. He glanced down the hall toward the door of Leslie's room. He hesitated for a moment before he turned and went out of the building without another comment.

Later, Ed questioned her about what Matt had said to her.

"He said that I was finding excuses because I wanted people to feel sorry for me," she said angrily. "And I do not have a martyr complex!"

Ed chuckled. "I know that."

"I can't believe you're related to someone like that," she said furiously. "He's horrible!"

"He's had a rough life. Something you can identify with," he added gently.

"I think he and his latest girlfriend deserve each other," she murmured.

"Carolyn phoned while he was here. I don't know what was said, but I'd bet my bottom dollar she denied saying anything to upset you."

"Would you expect her to admit it?" she asked. She laid back against the pillow, glad that the injection they'd given her was taking effect. "I guess I'll be clumping around your office in a cast for weeks, if he doesn't find some excuse to fire me in the meantime.''

''There is company policy in such matters,'' he said easily. ''He'd have to have my permission to fire you, and he won't get it.''

''I'm impressed,'' she said, and managed a wan smile.

''So you should be,'' he chuckled. He searched her eyes. ''Leslie, why didn't the doctor set those bones when it happened?''

She studied the ceiling. ''He said the whole thing was my fault and that I deserved all my wounds. He called me a vicious little tramp who caused decent men to be murdered.'' Her eyes closed. ''Nothing ever hurt so much.''

''I can imagine!''

''I never went to a doctor again,'' she continued. ''It wasn't just the things he said to me, you know. There was the expense, too. I had no insurance and no money. Mama had to have a public defender and I worked while I finished high school to help pay my way at my friend's house. The pain was bad, but eventually I got used to it, and the limp.'' She turned quiet eyes to Ed's face. ''It would be sort of nice to be able to walk normally again. And I will pay back whatever it costs, if you and your cousin will be patient.''

He winced. ''Nobody's worried about the cost.''

''He is,'' she informed him evenly. ''And he's

right. I don't want to be a financial burden on anyone, not even him.''

"We'll talk about all this later," he said gently. "Right now, I just want you to get better.''

She sighed. "Will I? I wonder.''

"Miracles happen all the time," he told her. "You're overdue for one.''

"I'd settle gladly for the ability to walk normally,'' she said at once, and she smiled.

Chapter Six

The operation was over by lunchtime the following day. Ed stayed until Leslie was out of the recovery room and out of danger, lying still and pale in the bed in the private room with the private nurse he'd hired to stay with her for the first couple of days. He'd spoken to both Lou Coltrain and the visiting orthopedic surgeon, who assured him that Miss Murry would find life much less painful from now on. Modern surgery had progressed to the point that procedures once considered impossible were now routine.

He went back to work feeling light and cheerful. Matt stopped him in the hall.

"Well?" he asked abruptly.

Ed grinned from ear to ear. "She's going to be fine. Dr. Santos said that in six weeks, when she comes out of that cast, she'll be able to dance in a contest."

Matt nodded. "Good."

Ed answered a question Matt had about one of their accounts and then, assuming that Matt didn't want anything else at the moment, he went back to his office. He had a temporary secretary, a pretty little redhead who had a bright personality and good dictation skills.

Surprisingly, Matt followed him into his office and closed the door. "Tell me how that bone was shattered," he said abruptly.

Ed sat down and leaned forward with his forearms on his cluttered desk. "That's Leslie's business, Matt," he replied. "I wouldn't tell you, even if I knew," he added, lying through his teeth with deliberate calm.

He sighed irritably. "She's a puzzle. A real puzzle."

"She's a sweet girl who's had a lot of hard knocks," Ed told him. "But regardless of what you think you know about her, she isn't 'easy.' Don't make the mistake of classing her with your usual sort of woman. You'll regret it."

Matt studied the younger man curiously and his eyes narrowed. "What do you mean, I think she's 'easy'?" he asked, bristling.

"Forgotten already? That's what you said about her."

Matt felt uncomfortable at the words that he'd spoken with such assurance to Leslie. He glanced at Ed irritably. "Miss Murry obviously means something to you. If you're so fond of her, why haven't you married her?"

Ed smoothed back his hair. "She kept me from blowing my brains out when my fiancée was gunned down in a bank robbery in Houston," he said. "I actually had the pistol loaded. She took it away from me."

Matt's eyes narrowed. "You never told me you were that despondent."

"You wouldn't have understood," came the reply. "Women were always a dime a dozen to you, Matt. You've never really been in love."

Matt's face, for once, didn't conceal his bitterness. "I wouldn't give any woman that sort of power over me," he said in clipped tones. "Women are devious, Ed. They'll smile at you until they get what they want, then they'll walk right over you to the next sucker. I've seen too many good men brought down by women they loved."

"There are bad men, too," Ed pointed out.

Matt shrugged. "I'm not arguing with that." He smiled. "I would have done what I could for you, though," he added. "We have our disagreements, but we're closer than most cousins are."

Ed nodded. "Yes, we are."

"You really are fond of Miss Murry, aren't you?"

"In a big brotherly sort of way," Ed affirmed. "She trusts me. If you knew her, you'd understand how difficult it is for her to trust a man."

"I think she's pulling the wool over your eyes," Matt told him. "You be careful. She's down on her luck, and you're rich."

Ed's face contorted briefly. "Good God, Matt, you haven't got a clue what she's really like."

"Neither have you," Matt commented with a cold smile. "But I know things about her that you don't. Let's leave it at that."

Ed hated his own impotence. "I want to keep her in my office."

"How do you expect her to come to work in a cast?" he asked frankly.

Ed leaned back in his chair and grinned. "The same way I did five years ago, when I had that skiing accident and broke my ankle. People work with broken bones all the time. And she doesn't type with her feet."

Matt shrugged. Miss Murry had him completely confused. "Suit yourself," he said finally. "Just keep her out of my way."

That shouldn't be difficult, Ed thought ruefully. Matt certainly wasn't on Leslie's list of favorite people. He wondered what the days ahead would bring. It would be like storing dynamite with lighted candles.

* * *

Leslie was out of the hospital in three days and back at work in a week. The company had paid for her surgery, to her surprise and Ed's. She knew that Matt had only done that out of guilt. Well, he needn't flay himself over what happened. She didn't really blame him. She had loved dancing with him. She refused to think of how that evening had ended. Some memories were best forgotten.

She hobbled into Ed's office with the use of crutches and plopped herself down behind her desk on her first day back on the job.

"How did you get here?" Ed asked with a surprised smile. "You can't drive, can you?"

"No, but one of the girls in my rooming house works in downtown Jacobsville and we're going to become a carpool three days a week. I'm paying my share of the gas and on her days off, I'll get a taxi to work," she added.

"I'm glad you're back," he said with genuine fondness.

"Oh, sure you are," she said with a teasing glance. "I heard all about Karla Smith when the girls from Mr. Caldwell's office came to see me. I understand she has a flaming crush on you."

Ed chuckled. "So they say. Poor girl."

She made a face. "You can't live in the past."

"Tell yourself that."

She put her crutches on the floor beside the desk, and swiveled back in her desk chair. "It's going to be a little difficult for me to get back and forth to your office," she said. "Can you dictate letters in here?"

"Of course."

She looked around the office with pleasure. "I'm glad I got to come back," she murmured. "I thought Mr. Caldwell might find an excuse to let me go."

"I'm Mr. Caldwell, too," he pointed out. "Matt's bark is worse than his bite. He won't fire you."

She grimaced. "Don't let me cause trouble between you," she said with genuine concern. "I'd rather quit…"

"No, you won't," he interrupted. He ruffled her short hair with a playful grin. "I like having you around. Besides, you spell better than the other women."

Her eyes lit up as she looked at him. She smiled back. "Thanks, boss."

Matt opened the door in time to encounter the affectionate looks they exchanged and his face hardened as he slammed it behind him.

They both jumped.

"Jehosophat, Matt!" Ed burst out, catching his breath. "Don't do that!"

"Don't play games with your secretary on my time," Matt returned. His cold dark eyes went to Leslie, whose own eyes went cold at sight of him. "Back at work, I see, Miss Murry."

"All the better to pay you back for my hospital stay, sir," she returned with a smile that bordered on insolence.

He bit back a sharp reply and turned to Ed, ignoring her. "I want you to take Nell Hobbs out to lunch and find out how she's going to vote on the zoning proposal. If they zone that land adjoining my ranch as recreational, I'm going to spend my life in court."

"If she votes for it, she'll be the only one," Ed assured him. "I spoke to the other commissioners myself."

He seemed to relax a little. "Okay. In that case, you can run over to Houlihan's dealership and drive my new Jaguar over here. It came in this morning."

Ed's eyes widened. "You're going to let me drive it?"

"Why not?" Matt asked with a warm smile, the sort Leslie knew she'd never see on that handsome face.

Ed chuckled. "Then, thanks. I'll be back shortly!" He started down the hall at a dead run. "Leslie, we'll do those letters after lunch!"

"Sure," she said. "I can spend the day updating those old herd records." She glanced at Matt to let him know she hadn't forgotten his instructions from before her operation.

He put his hands in the pockets of his slacks and his blue eyes searched her gray ones intently. Deliberately he let his gaze fall to her soft mouth. He remembered the feel of it clinging to his parted lips, hungry and moaning...

His teeth clenched. He couldn't think about that.

"The herd records can wait," he said tersely. "My secretary is home with a sick child, so you can work for me for the rest of the day. Ed can let Miss Smith handle his urgent stuff today."

She hesitated visibly. "Yes, sir," she said in a wooden voice.

"I have to talk to Henderson about one of the new accounts. I'll meet you in my office in thirty minutes."

"Yes, sir."

They were watching each other like opponents in a match when Matt made an angry sound under his breath and walked out.

Leslie spent a few minutes sorting the mail and looking over it. A little over a half hour went by before she realized it. A sound caught her attention and she looked up to find an impatient Matt Caldwell standing in the doorway.

"Sorry. I lost track of the time," she said quickly, putting the opened mail aside. She reached for her crutches and got up out of her chair, reaching for her pad and pen when she was ready to go. She looked up at Matt, who seemed taller than ever. "I'm ready when you are, boss," she said courteously.

"Don't call me boss," he said flatly.

"Okay, Mr. Caldwell," she returned.

He glared at her, but she gave him a bland look and even managed a smile. He wanted to throw things.

He turned, leaving her to follow him down the

long hall to his executive office, which had a bay window overlooking downtown Jacobsville. His desk was solid oak, huge, covered with equipment and papers of all sorts. There was a kid leather-covered chair behind the desk and two equally impressive wing chairs, and a sofa, all done in burgundy. The carpet was a deep, rich beige. The curtains were plaid, picking up the burgundy in the furniture and adding it to autumn hues. There was a framed portrait of someone who looked vaguely like Matt over the mantel of the fireplace, in which gas logs rested. There were two chairs and a table near the fireplace, probably where Matt and some visitor would share a pot of coffee or a drink. There was a bar against one wall with a mirror behind it, giving an added air of spacious comfort to the high-ceilinged room. The windows were tall ones, unused because the Victorian house that contained the offices had central heating.

Matt watched her studying her surroundings covertly. He closed the door behind them and motioned her into a chair facing the desk. She eased down into it and put her crutches beside her. She was still a little uncomfortable, but aspirin was enough to contain the pain these days. She looked forward to having the cast off, to walking normally again.

She put the pad on her lap and maneuvered the leg in the cast so that it was as comfortable as she could get it.

Matt was leaning back in his chair with his booted

feet on the desk and his eyes narrow and watchful as he sketched her slender body in the flowing beige pantsuit she was wearing with a patterned scarf tucked in the neck of the jacket. The outside seam in the left leg of her slacks had been snipped to allow for the cast. Otherwise, she was covered from head to toe, just as she had been from the first time he saw her. Odd, that he hadn't really noticed that before. It wasn't a new habit dating from the night he'd touched her so intimately, either.

"How's the leg?" he asked curtly.

"Healing, thank you," she replied. "I've already spoken to the bookkeeper about pulling out a quarter of my check weekly…"

He leaned forward so abruptly that it sounded like a gunshot when his booted feet hit the floor.

"I'll take that up with bookkeeping," he said sharply. "You've overstepped your authority, Miss Murry. Don't do it again."

She shifted in the chair, moving the ungainly cast, and assumed a calm expression. "I'm sorry, Mr. Caldwell."

Her voice was serene but her hands were shaking on the pad and pen. He averted his eyes and got to his feet, glaring out the window.

She waited patiently with her eyes on the blank pad, wondering when he was going to start dictation.

"You told Ed that Carolyn phoned you the night before we took you to the emergency room and made some cruel remarks." He remembered what Ed had related about that conversation and it made him unusually thoughtful. He turned and caught her surprised expression. "Carolyn denies saying anything to upset you."

Her expression didn't change. She didn't care what he thought of her anymore. She didn't say a word in her defense.

His dark eyebrows met over the bridge of his nose. "Well?"

"What would you like me to say?"

"You might try apologizing," he told her coldly, trying to smoke her out. "Carolyn was very upset to have such a charge made against her. I don't like having her upset," he added deliberately and stood looking down his nose at her, waiting for her to react to the challenge.

Her fingers tightened around the pencil. It was going to be worse than she ever dreamed, trying to work with him. He couldn't fire her, Ed had said, but that didn't mean he couldn't make her quit. If he made things difficult enough for her, she wouldn't be able to stay.

All at once, it didn't seem worth the effort. She was tired, worn-out, and Carolyn had hurt her, not the reverse. She was sick to death of trying to live from one day to the next with the weight of the past bearing down on her more each day. Being tormented by Matt Caldwell on top of all that was the last straw.

She reached for her crutches and stood up, pad and all.

"Where do you think you're going?" Matt demanded, surprised that she was giving up without an argument.

She went toward the door. He got in front of her, an easy enough task when every step she took required extreme effort.

She looked up at him with the eyes of a trapped animal, resigned and resentful and without life. "Ed said you couldn't fire me without his consent," she said quietly. "But you can hound me until I quit, can't you?"

He didn't speak. His face was rigid. "Would you give up so easily?" he asked, baiting her. "Where will you go?"

Her gaze dropped to the floor. Idly she noticed that one of her flat-heeled shoes had a smudge of mud on it. She should clean it off.

"I said, where will you go?" Matt persisted.

She met his cold eyes. "Surely in all of Texas, there's more than one secretarial position available," she said. "Please move. You're blocking the door."

He did move, but not in the way she'd expected. He took the crutches away from her and propped them against the bookshelf by the door. His hands went on either side of her head, trapping her in front of him. His dark eyes held a faint glitter as he studied her wan face, her soft mouth.

"Don't," she managed tightly.

He moved closer. He smelled of spice and after-shave and coffee. His breath was warm where it brushed her forehead. She could feel the warmth of his tall, fit body, and she remembered reluctantly how it had felt to let him hold her and touch her in his bedroom.

He was remembering those same things, but not with pleasure. He hated the attraction he felt for this woman, whom he didn't, couldn't trust.

"You don't like being touched, you said," he reminded her with deliberate sarcasm as his lean hand suddenly smoothed over her breast and settled there provocatively.

Her indrawn breath was audible. She looked up at him with all her hidden vulnerabilities exposed. "Please don't do this," she whispered. "I'm no threat to Ed, or to you, either. Just…let me go. I'll vanish."

She probably would, and that wounded him. He was making her life miserable. Why did this woman arouse such bitter feelings in him, when he was the soul of kindness to most people with problems—especially physical problems, like hers.

"Ed won't like it," he said tersely.

"Ed doesn't have to know anything," she said dully. "You can tell him whatever you like."

"Is he your lover?"

"No."

"Why not? You don't mind if he touches you."

"He doesn't. Not…the way you do."

Her strained voice made him question his own cruelty. He lifted his hand away from her body and tilted her chin up so that he could see her eyes. They were turbulent, misty.

"How many poor fools have you played the innocent with, Miss Murry?" he asked coldly.

She saw the lines in his face, many more than his age should have caused. She saw the coldness in his eyes, the bitterness of too many betrayals, too many loveless years.

Unexpectedly she reached up and touched his hair, smoothing it back as Lou had smoothed hers back in an act of silent compassion.

It made him furious. His body pressed down completely against hers, holding her prisoner. His hips twisted in a crude, rough motion that was instantly arousing.

She tried to twist away and he groaned huskily, giving her a worldly smile when she realized that her attempt at escape had failed and made the situation even worse.

Her face colored. It was like that night. It was the way Mike had behaved, twisting his body against her innocent one and laughing at her embarrassment. He'd said things, done things to her in front of his friends that still made her want to gag.

Matt's hand fell to her hip and contracted as he used one of his long legs to nudge hers apart. She was stiff against him, frozen with painful memories of another man, another encounter, that had begun just this way. She'd thought she loved Mike until he made her an object of lustful ridicule, making fun of her innocence as he anticipated its delights for the enjoyment of his laughing friends, grouped around them as he forcibly stripped the clothes away from her body. He laughed at her small breasts, at her slender figure, and all the while he touched her insolently and made jokes about her most intimate places.

She was years in the past, reliving the torment, the shame, that had seen her spread-eagled on the wood floor with Mike's drug-crazed friends each holding one of her shaking limbs still while Mike lowered his nude body onto hers and roughly parted her legs...

Matt realized belatedly that Leslie was frozen in place like a statue with a white face and eyes that didn't even see him. He could hear her heartbeat, quick and frantic. Her whole body shook, but not with pleasure or anticipation.

Frowning, he let her go and stepped back. She shivered again, convulsively. Mike had backed away, too, to the sound of a firecracker popping loudly. But it hadn't been a firecracker. It had been a bullet. It went right through him, into Leslie's leg. He looked surprised. Leslie remembered his blue eyes as the life visibly went out of them, leaving them fixed and blank just before he fell heavily on her. There had been such a tiny hole in his back, compared to the one in his chest. Her mother was screaming, trying

to fire again, trying to kill her. Leslie had seduced
her own lover, she wanted to kill them both, and she
was glad Mike was dead. Leslie would be dead, too!

Leslie remembered lying there naked on the floor,
with a shattered leg and blood pouring from it so
rapidly that she knew she was going to bleed to death
before help arrived...

"Leslie?" Matt asked sharply.

He became a white blur as she slid down the wall
into oblivion.

When she came to, Ed was bending over her with
a look of anguished concern. He had a damp towel
pressed to her forehead. She looked at him dizzily.

"Ed?" she murmured.

"Yes. How are you?"

She blinked and looked around. She was lying on
the big burgundy leather couch in Matt's office.
"What happened?" she asked numbly. "Did I
faint?"

"Apparently," Ed said heavily. "You came back
to work too soon. I shouldn't have agreed."

"But I'm all right," she insisted, pulling herself
up. She felt nauseous. She had to swallow repeatedly
before she was able to move again.

She took a slow breath and smiled at him. "I'm
still a little weak, I guess, and I didn't have any
breakfast."

"Idiot," he said, smiling.

She smiled back. "I'm okay. Hand me my crutches, will you?"

He got them from where they were propped against the wall, and she had a glimpse of Matt standing there as if he'd been carved from stone. She took the crutches from Ed and got them under her arms.

"Would you drive me home?" she asked Ed. "I think maybe I will take one more day off, if that's all right?"

"That's all right," Ed assured her. He looked across the room. "Right, Matt?"

Matt nodded, a curt jerk of his head. He gave her one last look and went out the door.

The relief Leslie felt almost knocked her legs from under her. She remembered what had happened, but she wasn't about to tell Ed. She wasn't going to cause a breach between him and the older cousin he adored. She, who had no family left in the world except the mother who hated her, had more respect for family than most people.

She let Ed take her home, and she didn't think about what had happened in Matt's office. She knew that every time she saw him from now on, she'd relive those last few horrible minutes in her mother's apartment when she was seventeen. If she'd had any-place else to go, she'd leave. But she was trapped, for the moment, at the mercy of a man who had none, a victim of a past she couldn't even talk about.

* * *

Ed went back to the office determined to have it out with Matt. He knew instinctively that Leslie's collapse was caused by something the other man did or said, and he was going to stop the treatment Matt was giving her before it was too late.

It was anticlimactic when he got into Matt's office, with his speech rehearsed and ready, only to find it empty.

"He said he was going up to Victoria to see a man about some property, Mr. Caldwell," one of the secretaries commented. "Left in a hurry, too, in that brand-new red Jaguar. We hear you got to drive it over from Houlihan's."

"Yes, I did," he replied, forcing a cheerful smile. "It goes like the wind."

"We noticed," she murmured dryly. "He was flying when he turned the corner. I hope he slows down. It would be a pity if he wrecked it when he'd only just gotten it."

"So it would," Ed replied. He went back to his own office, curious about Matt's odd behavior but rather relieved that the showdown wouldn't have to be faced right away.

Chapter Seven

Matt was doing almost a hundred miles an hour on the long highway that led to Victoria. He couldn't get Leslie's face out of his mind. That hadn't been anger or even fear in her gray eyes. It went beyond those emotions. She had been terrified; not of him, but of something she could see that he couldn't. Her tortured gaze had hurt him in a vulnerable spot he didn't know he had. When she fainted, he hated himself. He'd never thought of himself as a particularly cruel man, but he was with Leslie. He couldn't understand the hostility she roused in him. She was fragile, for all her independence and strength of will. Fragile. Vulnerable. Tender.

He remembered the touch of her soft fingers

smoothing back his hair and he groaned out loud with self-hatred. He'd been tormenting her, and she'd seen right through the harsh words to the pain that lay underneath them. In return for his insensitivity, she'd reached up and touched him with genuine compassion. He'd rewarded that exquisite tenderness with treatment he wouldn't have offered to a hardened prostitute.

He realized that the speed he was going exceeded the limit by a factor of two and took his foot off the pedal. He didn't even know where the hell he was going. He was running for cover, he supposed, and laughed coldly at his own reaction to Leslie's fainting spell. All his life he'd been kind to stray animals and people down on their luck. He'd followed up that record by torturing a crippled young woman who felt sorry for him. Next, he supposed, he'd be kicking lame dogs down steps.

He pulled off on the side of the highway, into a lay-by, and stopped the car, resting his head on the steering wheel. He didn't recognize himself since Leslie Murry had walked into his life. She brought out monstrous qualities in him. He was ashamed of the way he'd treated her. She was a sweet woman who always seemed surprised when people did kind things for her. On the other hand, Matt's antagonism and hostility didn't seem to surprise her. Was that what she'd had the most of in her life? Had people been so cruel to her that now she expected and accepted cruelty as her lot in life?

He leaned back in the seat and stared at the flat horizon. His mother's desertion and his recent notoriety had soured him on the whole female sex. His mother was an old wound. The assault suit had made him bitter, yet again, despite the fact that he'd avenged himself on the perpetrator. But he remembered her coy, sweet personality very well. She'd pretended innocence and helplessness and when the disguise had come off, he'd found himself the object of vicious public humiliation. His name had been cleared, but the anger and resentment had remained.

But none of that excused his recent behavior. He'd overreacted with Leslie. He was sorry and ashamed for making her suffer for something that wasn't her fault. He took a long breath and put the car in gear. Well, he couldn't run away. He might as well go back to work. Ed would probably be waiting with blood in his eye, and he wouldn't blame him. He deserved a little discomfort.

Ed did read him the riot act, and he took it. He couldn't deny that he'd been unfair to Leslie. He wished he could understand what it was about her that raised the devil in him.

"If you genuinely don't like her," Ed concluded, "can't you just ignore her?"

"Probably," Matt said without meeting his cousin's accusing eyes.

"Then would you? Matt, she needs this job," he continued solemnly.

Matt studied him sharply. "Why does she need it?" he asked. "And why doesn't she have anyplace to go?"

"I can't tell you. I gave my word."

"Is she in some sort of trouble with the law?"

Ed laughed softly. "Leslie?"

"Never mind." He moved back toward the door. He stopped and turned as he reached it. "When she fainted, she said something."

"What?" Ed asked curiously.

"She said, 'Mike, don't.'" He didn't blink. "Who's Mike?"

"A dead man," Ed replied. "Years dead."

"The man she and her mother competed for."

"That's right," Ed said. "If you mention his name in front of her, I'll walk out the door with her, and I won't come back. Ever."

That was serious business to Ed, he realized. He frowned thoughtfully. "Did she love him?"

"She thought she did," Ed replied. His eyes went cold. "He destroyed her life."

"How?"

Ed didn't reply. He folded his hands on the desk and just stared at Matt.

The older man let out an irritated breath. "Has it occurred to you that all this secrecy is only complicating matters?"

"It's occurred. But if you want answers, you'll have to ask Leslie. I don't break promises."

Matt muttered to himself as he opened the door

and went out. Ed stared after him worriedly. He hoped he'd done the right thing. He was trying to protect Leslie, but for all he knew, he might just have made matters worse. Matt didn't like mysteries. God forbid that he should try to force Leslie to talk about something she only wanted to forget. He was also worried about Matt's potential reaction to the old scandal. How would he feel if he knew how notorious Leslie really was, if he knew that her mother was serving a sentence for murder?

Ed was worried enough to talk to Leslie about it that evening when he stopped by to see how she was.

"I don't want him to know," she said when Ed questioned her. "Ever."

"What if he starts digging and finds out by himself?" Ed asked bluntly. "He'll read everyone's point of view except yours, and even if he reads every tabloid that ran the story, he still won't know the truth of what happened."

"I don't care what he thinks," she lied. "Anyway, it doesn't matter now."

"Why not?"

"Because I'm not coming back to work," she said evenly, avoiding his shocked gaze. "They need a typist at the Jacobsville sewing plant. I applied this afternoon and they accepted me."

"How did you get there?" he asked.

"Cabs run even in Jacobsville, Ed, and I'm not totally penniless." She lifted her head proudly. "I'll pay your cousin back the price of my operation, however long it takes. But I won't take one more day of the sort of treatment I've been getting from him. I'm sorry if he hates women, but I'm not going to become a scapegoat. I've had enough misery.''

"I'll agree there," he said. "But I wish you'd reconsider. I had a long talk with him…''

"You didn't tell him?'' she exclaimed, horrified.

"No, I didn't tell him," he replied. "But I think you should.''

"It's none of his business," she said through her teeth. "I don't owe him an explanation.''

"I know it doesn't seem like it, Leslie," he began, "but he's not a bad man." He frowned, searching for a way to explain it to her. "I don't pretend to understand why you set him off, but I'm sure he realizes that he's being unfair.''

"He can be unfair as long as he likes, but I'm not giving him any more free shots at me. I mean it, Ed. I'm not coming back.''

He leaned forward, feeling defeated. "Well, I'll be around if you need me. You're still my best friend.''

She reached out and touched his hand where it rested on his knee. "You're mine, too. I don't know how I'd have managed if it hadn't been for you and your father.''

He smiled. "You'd have found a way. Whatever you're lacking, it isn't courage.''

She sighed, looking down at her hand resting on his. "I don't know if that's true anymore," she confessed. "I'm so tired of fighting. I thought I could come to Jacobsville and get my life in order, get some peace. And the first man I run headlong into is a male chauvinist with a grudge against the whole female sex. I feel like I've been through the ringer backward."

"What did he say to you today?" he asked.

She blotted out the physical insult. "The usual things, most vividly the way I'd upset Carolyn by lying about her phone call."

"Some lie!" he muttered.

"He believes her."

"I can't imagine why. I used to think he was intelligent."

"He is, or he wouldn't be a millionaire." She got up. "Now go home, Ed. I've got to get some rest so I can be bright and cheerful my first day at my new job."

He winced. "I wanted things to be better than this for you."

She laughed gently. "And just think what a terrible world we'd have if we always got what we think we want."

He had to admit that she had a point. "That sewing plant isn't a very good place to work," he added worriedly.

"It's only temporary," she assured him.

He grimaced. "Well, if you need me, you know where I am."

She smiled. "Thanks."

* * *

He went home and ate supper and was watching the news when Matt knocked at the door just before opening it and walking in. And why not, Ed thought, when Matt had been raised here, just as he had. He grinned at his cousin as he came into the living room and sprawled over an easy chair.

"How does the Jag drive?" he asked.

"Like an airplane on the ground," he chuckled. He stared at the television screen for a minute. "How's Leslie?"

He grimaced. "She's got a new job."

Matt went very still. "What?"

"She said she doesn't want to work for me anymore. She got a job at the sewing plant, typing. I tried to talk her out of it. She won't budge." He glanced at Matt apologetically. "She knew I wouldn't let you fire her. She said you'd made sure she wanted to quit." He shrugged. "I guess you did. I've known Leslie for six years. I've never known her to faint."

Matt's dark eyes slid to the television screen and seemed to be glued there for a time. The garment company paid minimum wage. He doubted she'd have enough left over after her rent and grocery bill to pay for the medicine she had to take for pain. He couldn't remember a time in his life when he'd been so ashamed of himself. She wasn't going to like working in that plant. He knew the manager, a penny-pinching social climber who didn't believe in holidays, sick days, or paid vacation. He'd work her to death for her pittance and complain because she couldn't do more.

Matt's mouth thinned. He'd landed Leslie in hell with his bad temper and unreasonable prejudice.

Matt got up from the chair and walked out the door without a goodbye. Ed went back to the news without much real enthusiasm. Matt had what he wanted. He didn't look very pleased with it, though.

After a long night fraught with even more nightmares, Leslie got up early and took a cab to the manufacturing company, hobbling in on her crutches to the personnel office where Judy Blakely, the personnel manager, was waiting with her usual kind smile.

"Nice to see you, Miss Murry!"

"Nice to see you, too," she replied. "I'm looking forward to my new job."

Mrs. Blakely looked worried and reticent. She folded her hands in a tight clasp on her desk. "Oh, I don't know how to tell you this," she wailed. She grimaced. "Miss Murry, the girl you were hired to replace just came back a few minutes ago and begged me to let her keep her job. It seems she has serious family problems and can't do without her salary. I'm so sorry. If we had anything else open, even on the floor, I'd offer it to you temporarily. But we just don't."

The poor woman looked as if the situation tormented her. Leslie smiled gently. "Don't worry,

Mrs. Blakely, I'll find something else," she assured the older woman. "It's not the end of the world."

"I'd be furious," she said, her eyes wrinkled up with worry. "And you're being so nice...I feel like a dog!"

"You can't help it that things worked out like this." Leslie got to her feet a little heavily, still smiling. "Could you call me a cab?"

"Certainly! And we'll pay for it, too," she said firmly. "Honestly, I feel so awful!"

"It's all right. Sometimes we have setbacks that really turn into opportunities, you know."

Mrs. Blakely studied her intently. "You're such a positive person. I wish I was. I always seem to dwell on the negative."

"You might as well be optimistic, I always think," Leslie told her. "It doesn't cost extra."

Mrs. Blakely chuckled. "No, it doesn't, does it?" She phoned the cab and apologized again as Leslie went outside to wait for it.

She felt desolate, but she wasn't going to make that poor woman feel worse than she already did.

She was tired and sleepy. She wished the cab would come. She eased down onto the bench the company had placed out front for its employees, so they'd have a place to sit during their breaks. It was hard and uncomfortable, but much better than standing.

She wondered what she would do now. She had no prospects, no place to go. The only alternative was to look for something else or go back to Ed, and the latter choice wasn't a choice at all. She could never look Matt Caldwell in the face again without remembering how he'd treated her.

The sun glinted off the windshield of an approaching car, and she recognized Matt's new red Jaguar at once. She stood up, clutching her purse, stiff and defensive as he parked the car and got out to approach her.

He stopped an arm's length away. He looked as tired and worn-out as she did. His eyes were heavily lined. His black, wavy hair was disheveled. He put his hands on his hips and looked at her with pure malice.

She stared back with something approaching hatred.

"Oh, what the hell," he muttered, adding something about being hanged for sheep as well as lambs.

He bent and swooped her up in his arms and started walking toward the Jaguar. She hit him with her purse.

"Stop that," he muttered. "You'll make me drop you. Considering the weight of that damned cast, you'd probably sink halfway through the planet."

"You put me down!" she raged, and hit him again. "I won't go as far as the street with you!"

He paused beside the passenger door of the Jag and searched her hostile eyes. "I hate secrets," he said.

"I can't imagine you have any, with Carolyn shouting them to all and sundry!"

His eyes fell to her mouth. "I didn't tell Carolyn that you were easy," he said in a voice so tender that it made her want to cry.

Her lips trembled as she tried valiantly not to.

He made a husky sound and his mouth settled right on her misty eyes, closing them with soft, tender kisses.

She bawled.

He took a long breath and opened the passenger door, shifting her as he slid her into the low-slung vehicle. "I've noticed that about you," he murmured as he fastened her seat belt.

"Noticed…what?" she sobbed, sniffling.

He pulled a handkerchief out of his dress slacks and put it in her hands. "You react very oddly to tenderness."

He closed the door on her surprised expression and fetched her crutches before he went around to get in behind the wheel. He paused to fasten his own seat belt and give her a quick scrutiny before he started the powerful engine and pulled out into the road.

"How did you know I was here?" she asked when the tears stopped.

"Ed told me."

"Why?"

He shrugged. "Beats me. I guess he thought I might be interested."

"Fat chance!"

He chuckled. It was the first time she'd heard him laugh naturally, without mockery or sarcasm. He shifted gears. "You don't know the guy who owns that little enterprise," he said conversationally, "but the plant is a sweatshop."

"That isn't funny."

"Do you think I'm joking?" he replied. "He likes to lure illegal immigrants in here with promises of big salaries and health benefits, and then when he's got them where he wants them, he threatens them with the immigration service if they don't work hard and accept the pittance he pays. We've all tried to get his operation closed down, but he's slippery as an eel." He glanced at her with narrowed dark eyes. "I'm not going to let you sell yourself into that just to get away from me."

"Let me?" She rose immediately to the challenge, eyes flashing. "You don't tell me what to do!"

He grinned. "That's better."

She hit her hand against the cast, furious. "Where are you taking me?"

"Home."

"You're going the wrong way."

"My home."

"No," she said icily. "Not again. Not ever again!"

He shifted gears, accelerated, and shifted again. He loved the smoothness of the engine, the ride. He loved the speed. He wondered if Leslie had loved fast cars before her disillusionment.

He glanced at her set features. "When your leg heals, I'll let you drive it."

"No, thanks," she almost choked.

"Don't you like cars?"

She pushed back her hair. "I can't drive," she said absently.

"What?"

"Look out, you're going to run us off the road!" she squealed.

He righted the car with a muffled curse and down-shifted. "Everybody drives, for God's sake!"

"Not me," she said flatly.

"Why?"

She folded her arms over her breasts. "I just never wanted to."

More secrets. He was becoming accustomed to the idea that she never shared anything about her private life except, possibly, with Ed. He wanted her to open up, to trust him, to tell him what had happened to her. Then he laughed to himself at his own presumption. He'd been her mortal enemy since the first time he'd laid eyes on her, and he expected her to trust him?

"What are you laughing at?" she demanded.

He glanced at her as he slowed to turn into the ranch driveway. "I'll tell you one day. Are you hungry?"

"I'm sleepy."

He grimaced. "Let me see if I can guess why."

She glared at him. His own eyes had dark circles. "You haven't slept, either."

"Misery loves company."

"You started it!"

"Yes, I did!" he flashed back at her, eyes blazing. "Every time I look at you, I want to throw you down on the most convenient flat surface and ravish you! How's that for blunt honesty?"

She stiffened, wide-eyed, and gaped at him. He pulled up at his front door and cut off the engine. He turned in his seat and looked at her as if he resented her intensely. At the moment, he did.

His dark eyes narrowed. They were steady, intimidating. She glared into them.

But after a minute, the anger went out of him. He looked at her, really looked, and he saw things he hadn't noticed before. Her hair was dark just at her scalp. She was far too thin. Her eyes had dark circles so prominent that it looked as if she had two black eyes. There were harsh lines beside her mouth. She might pretend to be cheerful around Ed, but she wasn't. It was an act.

"Take a picture," she choked.

He sighed. "You really are fragile," he remarked quietly. "You give as good as you get, but all your vulnerabilities come out when you've got your back to the wall."

"I don't need psychoanalysis, but thanks for the thought," she said shortly.

He reached out, noticing how she shrank from his

touch. It didn't bother him now. He knew that it was tenderness that frightened her with him, not ardor. He touched her hair at her temple and brushed it back gently, staring curiously at the darkness that was more prevalent then.

"You're a brunette," he remarked. "Why do you color your hair?"

"I wanted to be a blonde," she replied instantly, trying to withdraw further against the door.

"You keep secrets, Leslie," he said, and for once he was serious, not sarcastic. "At your age, it's unusual. You're young and until that leg started to act up, you were even relatively healthy. You should be carefree. Your life is an adventure that's only just beginning."

She laughed hollowly. "I wouldn't wish my life even on you," she said.

He raised an eyebrow. "Your worst enemy," he concluded for her.

"That's right."

"Why?"

She averted her eyes to the windshield. She was tired, so tired. The day that had begun with such promise had ended in disappointment and more misery.

"I want to go home," she said heavily.

"Not until I get some answers out of you…!"

"You have no right!" she exploded, her voice breaking on the words. "You have no right, no right…!"

"Leslie!"

He caught her by the nape of the neck and pulled her face into his throat, holding her there even as she struggled. He smoothed her hair, her back, whispering to her, his voice tender, coaxing.

"What did I ever do to deserve you?" she sobbed. "I've never willingly hurt another human being in my life, and look where it got me! Years of running and hiding and never feeling safe…!"

He heard the words without understanding them, soothing her while she cried brokenly. It hurt him to hear her cry. Nothing had ever hurt so much.

He dried the tears and kissed her swollen, red eyes tenderly, moving to her temples, her nose, her cheeks, her chin and, finally, her soft mouth. But it wasn't passion that drove him now. It was concern.

"Hush, sweetheart," he whispered. "It's all right. It's all right!"

She must be dotty, she thought, if she was hearing endearments from Attila the Hun here. She sniffed and wiped her eyes again, finally getting control of herself. She sat up and he let her, his arm over the back of her seat, his eyes watchful and quiet.

She took a steadying breath and slumped in the seat, exhausted.

"Please take me home," she asked wearily.

He hesitated, but only for a minute. "If that's what you really want."

She nodded. He started the car and turned it around.

* * *

He helped her to the front door of the boarding-house, visibly reluctant to leave her.

"You shouldn't be alone in this condition," he said flatly. "I'll phone Ed and have him come over to see you."

"I don't need..." she protested.

His eyes flared. "The hell you don't! You need someone you can talk to. Obviously it isn't going to be your worst enemy, but then Ed knows all about you, doesn't he? You don't have secrets from him!"

He seemed to mind. She searched his angry face and wondered what he'd say if he knew those secrets. She gave him a lackluster smile.

"Some secrets are better kept," she said heavily. "Thanks for the ride."

"Leslie."

She hesitated, looking back at him.

His face looked harder than ever. "Were you raped?"

Chapter Eight

The words cut like a knife. She actually felt them. Her sad eyes met his dark, searching ones.

"Not quite," she replied tersely.

As understatements went, it was a master stroke. She watched the blood drain out of his face, and knew he was remembering, as she was, their last encounter, in his office, when she'd fainted.

He couldn't speak. He tried to, but the words choked him. He winced and turned away, striding back to the sports car. Leslie watched him go with a curious emptiness, as if she had no more feelings to bruise. Perhaps this kind detachment would last for a while, and she could have one day without the mental anguish that usually accompanied her, waking and sleeping.

She turned mechanically and went slowly into the house on her crutches, and down the hall to her small apartment. She had a feeling that she wouldn't see much of Matt Caldwell from now on. At last she knew how to deflect his pursuit. All it took was the truth—or as much of it as she felt comfortable letting him know.

Ed phoned to check on her later in the day and promised to come and see her the next evening. He did, arriving with a bag full of the Chinese take-out dishes she loved. While they were eating it, he mentioned that her job was still open.

"Miss Smith wouldn't enjoy hearing that," she teased lightly.

"Oh, Karla's working for Matt now."

She stared down at the wooden chopsticks in her hand. "Is she?"

"For some reason, he doesn't feel comfortable asking you to come back, so he sent me to do it," he replied. "He realizes that he's made your working environment miserable, and he's sorry. He wants you to come back and work for me."

She stared at him hard. "What did you tell him?"

"What I always tell him, that if he wants to know anything about you, he can ask you." He ate a forkful of soft noodles and took a sip of the strong coffee she'd brewed before he continued. "I gather he's realized that something pretty drastic happened to you."

"Did he say anything about it to you?"

"No." He lifted his gaze to meet hers. "He did go to the roadhouse out on the Victoria highway last night and wreck the bar."

"Why would he do something like that?" she asked, stunned by the thought of the straitlaced Mather Caldwell throwing things around.

"He was pretty drunk at the time," Ed confessed. "I had to bail him out of jail this morning. That was one for the books, let me tell you. The whole damned police department was standing around staring at him openmouthed when we left. He was only ever in trouble once, a woman accused him of assault—and he was cleared. His housekeeper testified that she'd been there the whole time and she and Matt had sent the baggage packing. But he's never treed a bar before."

She remembered the stark question he'd asked her and how she'd responded. She didn't understand why her past should matter to Matt. In fact, she didn't want to understand. He still didn't know the whole of it, and she was frightened of how he'd react if he knew. That wonderful tenderness he'd given her in the Jaguar had been actually painful, a bitter taste of what a man's love would be like. It was something she'd never experienced, and she'd better remember that Matt was the enemy. He'd felt sorry for her. He certainly wasn't in love with her. He wanted her, that was all. But despite her surprising response to his light caresses, complete physical intimacy was something she wasn't sure she was capable of responding to. The memories of Mike's vicious fondling made her sick. She couldn't live with them.

"Stop doing that to yourself," Ed muttered, dragging her back to the present. "You can't change the past. You have to walk straight into the future without flinching. It's the only way, to meet things head-on."

"Where did you learn that?" she asked.

"Actually I heard a televised sermon that caught my attention. That's what the minister said, that you have to go boldly forward and meet trouble head-on, not try to run away from it or hide." He pursed his lips. "I'd never heard it put quite that way before. It really made me think."

She sipped coffee with a sad face. "I've always tried to run. I've had to run." She lifted her eyes to his. "You know what they would have done to me if I'd stayed in Houston."

"Yes, I do, and I don't blame you for getting out while you could," Ed assured her. "But there's something I have to tell you now. And you're not going to like it."

"Don't tell me," she said with black humor, "someone from the local newspaper recognized me and wants an interview."

"Worse," he returned. "A reporter from Houston is down here asking questions. I think he's traced you."

She put her head in her hands. "Wonderful. Well, at least I'm no longer an employee of the Caldwell group, so it won't embarrass your cousin when I'm exposed."

"I haven't finished. Nobody will talk to him," he added with a grin. "In fact, he actually got into Matt's office yesterday when his secretary wasn't looking. He was only in there for a few minutes, and nobody knows what was said. But he came back out headfirst and, from what I hear, he ran out the door so fast that he left his briefcase behind with Matt cursing like a wounded sailor all the way down the hall. They said Matt had only just caught up with him at the curb when he ran across traffic and got away."

She hesitated. "When was this?"

"Yesterday." He smiled wryly. "It was a bad time to catch Matt. He'd already been into it with one of the county commissioners over a rezoning proposal we're trying to get passed, and his secretary had hidden in the bathroom to avoid him. That was how the reporter got in."

"You don't think he…told Matt?" she asked worriedly.

"No. I don't know what was said, of course, but he wasn't in there very long."

"But, the briefcase…"

"…was returned to him unopened," Ed said. "I know because I had to take it down to the front desk.'' He smiled, amused. ''I understand he paid someone to pick it up for him.''

''Thank God.''

''It was apparently the last straw for Matt, though,'' he continued, ''because it wasn't long after that when he said he was leaving for the day.''

''How did you know he was in jail?''

He grimaced. ''Carolyn phoned me. He'd come by her place first and apparently made inroads into a bottle of scotch. She hid the rest, after which he decided to go and get his own bottle.'' He shook his head. ''That isn't like Matt. He may have a drink or two occasionally, but he isn't a drinker. This has shocked everybody in town.''

''I guess so.'' She couldn't help but wonder if it had anything to do with the way he'd treated her. But if he'd gone to Carolyn, perhaps they'd had an argument and it was just one last problem on top of too many. ''Was Carolyn mad at him?'' she asked.

''Furious,'' he returned. ''Absolutely seething. It seems they'd had a disagreement of major proportions, along with all the other conflicts of the day.'' He shook his head. ''Matt didn't even come in to work today. I'll bet his head is splitting.''

She didn't reply. She stared into her coffee with dead eyes. Everywhere she went, she caused trouble. Hiding, running—nothing seemed to help. She was only involving innocent people in her problems.

Ed hesitated when he saw her face. He didn't want

to make things even worse for her, but there was more news that he had to give her.

She saw that expression. "Go ahead," she invited. "One more thing is all I need right now, on top of being crippled and jobless."

"Your job is waiting," he assured her. "Whenever you want to come in."

"I won't do that to him," she said absently. "He's had enough."

His eyes became strangely watchful. "Feeling sorry for the enemy?" he asked gently.

"You can't help not liking people," she replied. "He likes most everybody except me. He's basically a kind person. I just rub him the wrong way."

He wasn't going to touch that line. "The same reporter who came here had gone to the prison to talk to your mother," he continued. "I was concerned, so I called the warden. It seems…she's had a heart attack."

Her heart jumped unpleasantly. "Will she live?"

"Yes," he assured her. "She's changed a lot in six years, Leslie," he added solemnly. "She's reconciled to serving her time. The warden says that she wanted to ask for you, but that she was too ashamed to let them contact you. She thinks you can't ever forgive what she said and did to you."

Her eyes misted, but she fought tears. Her mother had been eloquent at the time, with words and the pistol. She stared at her empty coffee cup. "I can forgive her. I just don't want to see her."

"She knows that," Ed replied.

She glanced at him. "Have you been to see her?"

He hesitated. Then he nodded. "She was doing very well until this reporter started digging up the past. He was the one who suggested the movie deal and got that bit started." He sighed angrily. "He's young and ambitious and he wants to make a name for himself. The world's full of people like that, who don't care what damage they do to other peoples' lives as long as they get what they want."

She was only vaguely listening. "My mother...did she ask you about me?"

"Yes."

"What did you tell her?" she wanted to know.

He put down his cup. "The truth. There really wasn't any way to dress it up." His eyes lifted. "She wanted you to know that she's sorry for what happened, especially for the way she treated you before and after the trial. She understands that you don't want to see her. She says she deserves it for destroying your life."

She stared into space with the pain of memory eating at her. "She was never satisfied with my father," she said quietly. "She wanted things he couldn't give her, pretty clothes and jewelry and nights on the town. All he knew how to do was fly a crop-dusting plane, and it didn't pay much..." Her eyes closed. "I saw him fly into the electrical wires, and go down," she whispered gruffly. "I saw him go down!" Her eyes began to glitter with feeling. "I knew he was dead before they ever got to him. I ran home. She was in the living room, playing music, dancing. She didn't care. I broke the record player and threw myself at her, screaming.''

Ed grimaced as she choked, paused, and fought for control. ''We were never close, especially after the funeral,'' she continued, ''but we were stuck with each other. Things went along fairly well. She got a job waiting tables and made good tips when she was working. She had trouble holding down a job because she slept so much. I got a part-time job typing when I was sixteen, to help out. Then when I'd just turned seventeen, Mike came into the restaurant and started flirting with her. He was so handsome, well-bred and had nice manners. In no time, he'd moved in with us. I was crazy about him, you know the way a young girl has crushes on older men. He teased me, too. But he had a drug habit that we didn't know about. She didn't like him teasing me, anyway, and she had a fight with him about it. The next day, he had some friends over and they all got high.'' She shivered. ''The rest you know.''

''Yes.'' He sighed, studying her wan face.

''All I wanted was for her to love me,'' she said dully. ''But she never did.''

''She said that,'' he replied. ''She's had a lot of time to live with her regrets.'' He leaned forward to search her eyes. ''Leslie, did you know that she had a drug habit?''

''She what?'' she exclaimed, startled.

"Had a drug habit," he repeated. "That's what she told me. It was an expensive habit, and your father got tired of trying to support it. He loved her, but he couldn't make the sort of money it took to keep her high. It wasn't clothes and jewelry and parties. It was drugs."

She felt as if she'd been slammed to the floor. She moved her hands over her face and pushed back her hair. "Oh, Lord!"

"She was still using when she walked in on Mike and his friends holding you down," he continued.

"How long had she been using drugs?" she asked.

"A good five years," he replied. "Starting with marijuana and working her way up to the hard stuff."

"I had no idea."

"And you didn't know that Mike was her dealer, either, apparently."

She gasped.

He nodded grimly. "She told me that when I went to see her, too. She still can't talk about it easily. Now that she has a good grip on reality, she sees what her life-style did to you. She had hoped that you might be married and happy by now. It hurt her deeply to realize that you don't even date."

"She'll know why, of course," she said bitterly.

"You sound so empty, Leslie."

"I am." She leaned back. "I don't care if the reporter finds me. It doesn't matter anymore. I'm so tired of running."

"Then stand and deliver," he replied, getting to

his feet. "Come back to work. Let your leg heal. Let your hair grow out and go back to its natural color. Start living."

"Can I, after so long?"

"Yes," he assured her. "We all go through periods of anguish, times when we think we can't face what lies ahead. But the only way to get past it is to go through it, straight through it. No detours, no camouflage, no running. You have to meet problems head-on, despite the pain."

She cocked her head and smiled at him with real affection. "Were you ever a football coach?"

He chuckled. "I hate contact sports."

"Me, too." She brushed her short hair back with her hands. "Okay. I'll give it a shot. But if your cousin gives me any more trouble…"

"I don't think Matt is going to cause you any more problems," he replied.

"Then, I'll see you on Thursday morning."

"Thursday? Tomorrow is just Wednesday…"

"Thursday," she said firmly. "I have plans for tomorrow."

And she did. She had the color taken out of her hair at a local beauty salon. She took her contact lenses to the local optometrist and got big-lensed, wire-framed glasses to wear. She bought clothes that looked professional without being explicit.

Then, Thursday morning, cast and crutches notwithstanding, she went back to work.

She'd been at her desk in Ed's office for half an hour when Matt came in. He barely glanced at her, obviously not recognizing the new secretary, and tapped on Ed's door, which was standing open.

"I'm going to fly to Houston for the sale," he told Ed. He sounded different. His deep voice held its usual authority, but there was an odd note in it. "I don't suppose you were able to convince her to come back...why are you shaking your head?"

Ed stood up with an exasperated sigh and pointed toward Leslie.

Matt scowled, turning on his heel. He looked at her, scowled harder, moved closer, peering into her upturned face.

She saw him matching his memory of her with the new reality. She wondered how she came off, but it was far too soon to get personal.

His eyes went over her short dark hair, over the feminine but professional beige suit she was wearing with a tidy patterned blouse, lingering on the glasses that she'd never worn before in his presence. His own face was heavily lined and he looked as if he'd had his own share of turmoil since she'd seen him last. Presumably he was still having problems with Carolyn.

"Good morning, Miss Murry," he murmured. His eyes didn't smile at her. He looked as if his face was painted on.

That was odd. No sarcasm, no mockery. No insolent sizing up. He was polite and courteous to a fault.

If that was the way he intended to play it…

"Good morning, Mr. Caldwell," she replied with equal courtesy.

He studied her for one long moment before he turned back to Ed. "I should be back by tonight. If I'm not, you'll have to meet with the county commission and the zoning committee."

"Oh, no," Ed groaned.

"Just tell them we're putting up a two-story brick office building on our own damned land, whether they like it or not," Matt told him, "and that we can accommodate them in court for as many years as it takes to get our way. I'm tired of trying to do business in a hundred-year-old house with frozen pipes that burst every winter."

"It won't sound as intimidating if I say it."

"Stand in front of a mirror and practice looking angry."

"Is that how you did it?" Ed murmured dryly.

"Only at first," he assured the other man, deadpan. "Just until I got the hang of it."

"I remember," Ed chuckled. "Even Dad wouldn't argue with you unless he felt he had a good case."

Matt shoved his hands into his pockets. "If you need me, you know the cell phone number."

"Sure."

Still he hesitated. He turned and glanced at Leslie, who was opening mail. The expression on his face fascinated Ed, who'd known him most of his life. It wasn't a look he recognized.

Matt started out the door and then paused to look back at Leslie, staring at her until she lifted her eyes.

He searched them slowly, intently. He didn't smile. He didn't speak. Her cheeks became flushed and she looked away. He made an awkward movement with his shoulders and went out the door.

Ed joined her at her desk when Matt was out of sight. "So far, so good," he remarked.

"I guess he really doesn't mind letting me stay," she murmured. Her hands were shaking because of that long, searching look of Matt's. She clasped them together so that Ed wouldn't notice and lifted her face. "But what if that reporter comes back?"

He pursed his lips. "Odd, that. He left town yesterday. In a real hurry, too. The police escorted him to the city limits and the sheriff drove behind him to the county line."

She gaped at him.

He shrugged. "Jacobsville is a small, close-knit community and you just became part of it. That means," he added, looking almost as imposing as his cousin, "that we don't let outsiders barge in and start harassing our citizens. I understand there's an old city law still on the books that makes it a crime for anyone to stay in a local place of lodging unless he or she is accompanied by at least two pieces of luggage or a trunk." He grinned. "Seems the reporter only had a briefcase. Tough."

"He might come back with a trunk and two suitcases," she pointed out.

He shook his head. "It seems that they found another old law which makes it illegal for a man driving a rental car to park it anywhere inside the city limits. Strange, isn't it, that we'd have such an unusual ordinance."

Leslie felt the first ripple of humor that she'd experienced for weeks. She smiled. "My, my."

"Our police chief is related to the Caldwells," he explained. "So is the sheriff, one of the county commissioners, two volunteer firemen, a sheriff's deputy and a Texas Ranger who was born here and works out of Fort Worth." He chuckled. "The governor is our second cousin."

Her eyes widened. "No Washington connections?" she asked.

"Nothing major. The vice president is married to my aunt."

"Nothing major." She nodded. She let out her breath. "Well, I'm beginning to feel very safe."

"Good. You can stay as long as you like. Permanently, as far as I'm concerned."

She couldn't quite contain the pleasure it gave her to feel as if she belonged somewhere, a place where she was protected and nurtured and had friends. It was a first for her. Her eyes stung with moisture.

"Don't start crying," Ed said abruptly. "I can't stand it."

She swallowed and forced a watery smile to her

lips. ''I wasn't going to,'' she assured him. She moved her shoulders. ''Thanks,'' she said gruffly.

''Don't thank me,'' he told her. ''Matt rounded up the law enforcement people and had them going through dusty volumes of ordinances to find a way to get that reporter out of here.''

''Matt did?''

He held up a hand as she started to parade her misgivings about what he might have learned of her past. ''He doesn't know why the man was here. It was enough that he was asking questions about you. You're an employee. We don't permit harassment.''

''I see.''

She didn't, but that was just as well. The look Ed had accidentally seen on Matt's face had him turning mental cartwheels. No need to forewarn Leslie. She wasn't ever going to have to worry about being hounded again, not if he knew Matt. And he didn't believe for one minute that his cousin was flying all the way to Houston for a cattle sale that he usually wouldn't be caught dead at. The foreman at his ranch handled that sort of thing, although Leslie didn't know. Ed was betting that Matt had another reason for going to Houston, and it was to find out who hired that reporter and sent him looking for Leslie. He felt sorry for the source of that problem. Matt in a temper was the most menacing human being he'd ever known. He didn't rage or shout and he usually didn't hit, but he had wealth and power and he knew how to use them.

He went back into his office, suddenly worried despite the reassurances he'd given Leslie. Matt didn't know why the reporter was digging around, but what if he found out? He would only be told what the public had been told, that Leslie's mother had shot her daughter and her live-in lover in a fit of jealous rage and that she was in prison. He might think, as others had, that Leslie had brought the whole sordid business on herself by having a wild party with Mike and his friends, and he wouldn't be sympathetic. More than likely, he'd come raging back home and throw Leslie out in the street. Furthermore, he'd have her escorted to the county line like the reporter who'd been following her.

He worried himself sick over the next few hours. He couldn't tell Leslie, when he might only be worrying for nothing. But the thought haunted him that Matt was every bit as dogged as a reporter when it came to ferreting out facts.

In the end, he phoned a hotel that Matt frequented when he was in Houston overnight and asked for his room. But when he was connected, it wasn't Matt who answered the phone.

"Carolyn?" Ed asked, puzzled. "Is Matt there?"

"Not right now," came the soft reply. "He had an appointment to see someone. I suppose he's forgotten that I'm waiting for him with this trolley full of food. I suppose it will be cold as ice by the time he turns up."

"Everything's all right, isn't it?"

"Why wouldn't it be?" she teased.

"Matt's been acting funny."

"Yes, I know. That Murry girl!" Her indrawn breath was audible. "Well, she's caused quite enough trouble. When Matt comes back, she'll be right out of that office, let me tell you! Do you have any idea what that reporter told Matt about her...?"

Ed hung up, sick. So not only did Matt know, but Carolyn knew, too. She'd savage Leslie, given the least opportunity. He had to do something. What?

Ed didn't expect Matt that evening, and he was right. Matt didn't come back in time for the county commission meeting, and Ed was forced to go in his place. He held his own, as Matt had instructed him to, and got what he wanted. Then he went home, sitting on pins and needles as he waited for someone to call him—either Leslie, in tears, or Matt, in a temper.

But the phone didn't ring. And when he went into work the next morning, Leslie was sitting calmly at her desk typing the letters he'd dictated to her just before they closed the day before.

"How did the meeting go?" she asked at once.

"Great," he replied. "Matt will be proud of me." He hesitated. "He, uh, isn't in yet, is he?"

"No. He hasn't phoned, either." She frowned. "You don't suppose anything went wrong with the plane, do you?"

She sounded worried. Come to think of it, she looked worried, too. He frowned. "He's been flying for a long time," he pointed out.

"Yes, but there was a bad storm last night." She hesitated. She didn't want to worry, but she couldn't help it. Despite the hard time he'd given her, Matt had been kind to her once or twice. He wasn't a bad person; he just didn't like her.

"If anything had happened, I'd have heard by now," he assured her. His lips pursed as he searched for the words. "He didn't go alone."

Her heart stopped in her chest. "Carolyn?"

He nodded curtly. He ran a hand through his hair. "He knows, Leslie. They both do."

She felt the life ebb out of her. But what had she expected, that Matt would wait to hear her side of the story? He was the enemy. He wouldn't for one second believe that she was the victim of the whole sick business. How could she blame him?

She turned off the word processor and moved her chair back, reaching for her purse. She felt more defeated than she ever had in her life. One bad break after another, she was thinking, as she got to her feet a little clumsily.

"Hand me my crutches, Ed, there's a dear," she said steadily.

"Oh, Leslie," he groaned.

She held her hand out and, reluctantly, he helped her get them in place.

"Where will you go?" he asked.

She shrugged. "It doesn't matter. Something will turn up."

"I can help."

She looked up at him with sad resignation. "You can't go against your own blood kin, Ed," she replied. "I'm the outsider here. And one way or another, I've already caused too much trouble. See you around, pal. Thanks for everything."

He sighed miserably. "Keep in touch, at least."

She smiled. "Certainly I'll do that. See you."

He watched her walk away with pure anguish. He wished he could make her stay, but even he wouldn't wish that on her. When Matt came home, he'd be out for blood. At least she'd be spared that confrontation.

Chapter Nine

Leslie didn't have a lot to pack, only a few clothes and personal items, like the photograph of her father that she always carried with her. She'd bought a bus ticket to San Antonio, one of the places nosy reporters from Houston might not think to look for her. She could get a job as a typist and find another place to live. It wouldn't be so bad.

She thought about Matt, and how he must feel, now that he knew the whole truth, or at least, the reporter's version of it. She was sure that he and Carolyn would have plenty to gossip about on the way back home. Carolyn would broadcast the scandal all over town. Even if Leslie stopped working for Matt, she would never live down the gossip. Leaving was her only option.

Running away. Again.

Her hands went to a tiny napkin she'd brought home from the dance that she and Ed had attended with Matt and Carolyn. Matt had been doodling on it with his pen just before he'd pulled Leslie out of her seat and out onto the dance floor. It was a silly sentimental piece of nonsense to keep. On a rare occasion or two, Matt had been tender with her. She wanted to remember those times. It was good to have had a little glimpse of what love might have been like, so that life didn't turn her completely bitter.

She folded her coat over a chair and looked around to make sure she wasn't missing anything. She wouldn't have time to look in the morning. The bus would leave at 6:00 a.m., with or without her. She clumped around the apartment with forced cheer, thinking that at least she'd have no knowing, pitying smiles in San Antonio.

Ed looked up as Matt exploded into the office, stopping in his tracks when he reached Leslie's empty desk. He stood there, staring, as if he couldn't believe what he was seeing.

With a sigh, Ed got up and joined him in the outer office, steeling himself for the ordeal. Matt was obviously upset.

"It's all right," he told Matt. "She's already gone. She said she was sorry for the trouble she'd caused, and that…"

"Gone?" Matt looked horrified. His face was like white stone.

Ed frowned, hesitating. "She said it would spare you the trouble of firing her," he began uneasily.

Matt still hadn't managed a coherent sentence. He ran his hand through his hair, disturbing its neat wave. He stuck his other hand into his pocket and went on staring at her desk as if he expected she might materialize out of thin air if he looked hard enough.

He turned to Ed. He stared at him, almost as if he didn't recognize him. "She's gone. Gone where?"

"She wouldn't tell me," he replied reluctantly.

Matt's eyes were black. He looked back at her desk and winced. He made a violent motion, pressed his lips together, and suddenly took a deep audible breath and with a furious scowl, he let out a barrage of nonstop curses that had even Ed gaping.

"...and I did *not* say she could leave!" he finished at the end.

Ed managed to meet those flashing eyes, but it wasn't easy. Braver men than he had run for cover when the boss lost his temper. "Now, Matt..."

"Don't you 'Now, Matt' me, dammit!" he raged. His fists were clenched at his sides and he looked as if he really wanted to hit something. Or someone. Ed took two steps backward.

Matt saw two of the secretaries standing frozen in the hall, as if they'd come running to find the source of the uproar and were now hoping against hope that it wouldn't notice them.

No such luck. "Get the hell back to work!" he shouted.

They actually ran.

Ed wanted to. "Matt," he tried again.

He was talking to thin air. Matt was down the hall and out the door before he could catch up. He did the only thing he could. He rushed back to his office to phone Leslie and warn her. He was so nervous that it took several tries and one wrong number to get her.

"He's on his way over there," Ed told her the minute she picked up the phone. "Get out."

"No."

"Leslie, I've never seen him like this," he pleaded. "You don't understand. He isn't himself."

"It's all right, Ed," she said calmly. "There's nothing more he can do to me."

"Leslie…!" he groaned.

The loud roar of an engine out front caught her attention. "Try not to worry," she told Ed, and put the receiver down on an even louder exclamation.

She got up, put her crutches in place and hobbled to open her door just as Matt started to knock on it. He paused there, his fist upraised, his eyes black in a face the color of rice.

She stood aside to let him in, with no sense of self-preservation left. She was as far down as she could get already.

He closed the door behind him with an ultracontrolled softness before he turned to look at her. She went back to her armchair and eased down into it, laying the crutches to one side. Her chin lifted and she just looked at him, resigned to more verbal abuse if not downright violence. She was already packed and almost beyond his reach. Let him do his worst.

Now that he was here, he didn't know what to do. He hadn't thought past finding her. He leaned back against the door and folded his arms over his chest.

She didn't flinch or avert her eyes. She stared right at him. "There was no need to come here," she said calmly. "You don't have to run me out of town. I already have my ticket. I'm leaving on the bus first thing in the morning." She lifted a hand. "Feel free to search if you think I've taken anything from the office."

He didn't respond. His chest rose and fell rhythmically, if a little heavily.

She smoothed her hand over the cast where it topped her kneecap. There was an itch and she couldn't get to it. What a mundane thing to think about, she told herself, when she was confronted with a homicidal man.

He was making her more nervous by the minute. She shifted in the chair, grimacing as the cast moved awkwardly and gave her a twinge of pain.

"Why are you here?" she asked impatiently, her eyes flashing at him through her lenses. "What else do you want, an apology...?"

"An apology? Dear God!"

It sounded like a plea for salvation. He moved, for the first time, going slowly across the room to the chair a few feet away from hers, next to the window. He eased himself down into it and crossed his long legs. He was still scowling, watching, waiting.

His eyes were appraising her now, not cutting into her or mocking her. They were dark and steady and turbulent.

Her eyes were dull and lackluster as she averted her face. Her grip on the arm of the chair was painful. "You know, don't you?"

"Yes."

She felt as if her whole body contracted. She watched a bird fly past the window and wished that she could fly away from her problems. "In a way, it's sort of a relief," she said wearily. "I'm so tired...of running."

His face tautened. His mouth made a thin line as he stared at her. "You'll never have to run again," he said flatly. "There isn't going to be any more harassment from that particular quarter."

She wasn't sure she was hearing right. Her face turned back to his. It was hard to meet those searching eyes, but she did. He looked pale, worn.

"Why aren't you gloating?" she asked harshly. "You were right about me all along, weren't you? I'm a little tramp who lures men in and teases them...!"

"Don't!" He actually flinched. He searched for

words and couldn't manage to find anything to say to her. His guilt was killing him. His conscience had him on a particularly nasty rack. He looked at her and saw years of torment and self-contempt, and he wanted to hit something.

That expression was easily read in his dark eyes. She leaned her head back against the chair and closed her eyes on the hatred she saw there.

"Everybody had a different idea of why I did it," she said evenly. "One of the bigger tabloids even interviewed a couple of psychiatrists who said I was getting even with my mother for my childhood. Another said it was latent nymphomania…"

"Hell!"

She felt dirty. She couldn't look at him. "I thought I loved him," she said, as if even after all the years, she still couldn't believe it had happened. "I had no idea, none at all, what he was really like. He made fun of my body, he and his friends. They stretched me out like a human sacrifice and discussed… my…assets." Her voice broke. He clenched his hand on the arm of the chair.

Matt's expression, had she seen it, would have silenced her. As it was, she was staring blankly out the window.

"They decided Mike should go first," she said in a husky, strained tone. "And then they drew cards to see which of the other three would go next. I prayed to die. But I couldn't. Mike was laughing at the way I begged him not to do it. I struggled and he had the others hold me down while he…''

A sound came from Matt's tight throat that shocked her into looking at him. She'd never seen such horror in a man's eyes.

''My mother came in before he had time to—'' she swallowed ''—get started. She was so angry that she lost control entirely. She grabbed the pistol Mike kept in the table drawer by the front door and she shot him. The bullet went through him and into my leg,'' she whispered, sickened by the memory. ''I saw his face when the bullet hit him in the chest from behind. I actually saw the life drain out of him.'' She closed her eyes. ''She kept shooting until one of the men got the pistol away from her. They ran for their lives, and left us there, like that. A neighbor called an ambulance and the police. I remember that one of them got a blanket from the bedroom and wrapped me up in it. They were all…so kind,'' she choked, tears filling her eyes. ''So kind!''

He put his face in his hands. He couldn't bear what he was hearing. He remembered her face in his office when he'd laughed at her. He groaned harshly.

''The tabloids made it look as if I'd invited what happened,'' she said huskily. ''I don't know how a seventeen-year-old virgin can ask grown men to get high on drugs and treat her with no respect. I thought I loved Mike, but even so, I never did anything consciously to make him treat me that way.''

Matt couldn't look at her. Not yet. ''People high

on drugs don't know what they're doing, as a rule,'' he said through his teeth.

''That's hard to believe,'' she said.

''It's the same thing as a man drinking too much alcohol and having a blackout,'' he said, finally lifting his head. He stared at her with dark, lifeless eyes. ''Didn't I tell you once that secrets are dangerous?''

She nodded. She looked back out the window. ''Mine was too sordid to share,'' she said bitterly. ''I can't bear to be touched by men. By most men,'' she qualified. ''Ed knew all about me, so he never approached me, that way. But you,'' she added quietly, ''came at me like a bull in a pasture. You scared me to death. Aggression always reminds me of…of Mike.''

He leaned forward with his head bowed. Even after what he'd learned in Houston already, he was unprepared for the full impact of what had been done to this vulnerable, fragile creature in front of him. He'd let hurt pride turn him into a predator. He'd approached her in ways that were guaranteed to bring back terrible memories of that incident in her past.

''I wish I'd known,'' he said heavily.

''I don't blame you,'' she said simply. ''You couldn't have known.''

His dark eyes came up glittering. ''I could have,'' he contradicted flatly. ''It was right under my nose. The way you downplayed your figure, the way you backed off when I came too close, the way you…fainted—'' he had to force the word out ''—in my office when I pinned you to the wall.'' He looked away. ''I didn't see it because I didn't want to. I was paying you back,'' he said on a bitter laugh, ''for having the gall not to fall into my arms when I pursued you.''

She'd never imagined that she could feel sorry for Matt Caldwell. But she did. He was a decent man. Surely it would be difficult for him to face the treatment he'd given her, now that he knew the truth.

She smoothed her hands over her arms. It wasn't cold in the room, but she was chilled.

''You've never talked about it, have you?'' he asked after a minute.

''Only to Ed, right after it happened,'' she replied. ''He's been the best friend in the world to me. When those people started talking about making a television movie of what had happened, I just panicked. They were all over Houston looking for me. Ed offered me a way out and I took it. I was so scared,'' she whispered. ''I thought I'd be safe here.''

His fists clenched. ''Safe.'' He made a mockery of the very word.

He got to his feet and moved to the window, avoiding her curious gaze.

''That reporter,'' she began hesitantly. ''He told you about it when he was here, didn't he?''

He didn't reply for a minute. ''Yes,'' he said finally. ''He had clippings of the story.'' She probably knew which ones, he thought miserably, of her being carried out on a stretcher with blood all over her.

There was one of the dead man lying on the floor of the apartment, and one of her blond mother shocked and almost catatonic as policemen escorted her to the squad car.

"I didn't connect it when you told Ed you were going to Houston. I thought it was some cattle sale, just like you said," she remarked.

"The reporter ran, but he'd already said that he was working with some people in Hollywood trying to put together a television movie. He'd tried to talk to your mother, apparently, and after his visit, she had a heart attack. That didn't even slow him down. He tracked you here and had plans to interview you." He glanced at her. "He thought you'd be glad to cooperate for a percentage of the take."

She laughed hollowly.

"Yes, I know," he told her. "You're not mercenary. That's one of the few things I've learned about you since you've been here."

"At least you found one thing about me that you like," she told him.

His face closed up completely. "There are a lot of things I like about you, but I've had some pretty hard knocks from women in my life."

"Ed told me."

"It's funny," he said, but he didn't look amused. "I've never been able to come to terms with my mother's actions—until I met you. You've helped me a lot—and I've been acting like a bear with a thorn in its paw. I've mistreated you."

She searched his lean, hard face quietly. He was so handsome. Her heart jumped every time she met his eyes. "Why did you treat me that way?" she asked.

He stuck his hand into his pocket. "I wanted you," he said flatly.

"Oh."

She wasn't looking at him, but he saw her fingers curl into the arm of the chair. "I know. You probably aren't capable of desire after what was done to you. Perhaps it's poetic justice that my money and position won't get me the one thing in the world I really want."

"I don't think I could sleep with someone," she agreed evenly. "Even the thought of it is...disgusting."

He could imagine that it was, and he cursed that man silently until he ran out of words.

"You liked kissing me."

She nodded, surprised. "Yes, I did."

"And being touched," he prompted, smiling gently at the memory of her reaction—astonishing now, considering her past.

She studied her lap. A button on her dress was loose. She'd have to stitch it. She lifted her eyes. "Yes," she said. "I enjoyed that, too, at first."

His face hardened as he remembered what he'd said to her then. He turned away, his back rigid. He'd made so damned many mistakes with this woman that he didn't know how he was going to make amends. There was probably no way to do it. But he could protect her from any more misery, and he was going to.

He rammed his hands into his pockets and turned. "I went to see that reporter in Houston. I can promise you that he won't be bothering you again, and there won't be any more talk of a motion picture. I went to see your mother, too," he added.

She hadn't expected that. She closed her eyes. She caught her lower lip in her teeth and bit it right through. The taste of blood steeled her as she waited for the explosion.

"Don't!"

She opened her eyes with a jerk. His face was dark and lined, like the downwardly slanted brows above his black eyes. She pulled a tissue from the box on the table beside her and dabbed at the blood on her lip. It was such a beautiful color, she thought irrelevantly.

"I didn't realize how hard this was going to be," he said, sitting down. His head bowed, he clasped his big hands between his splayed knees and stared at the floor. "There are a lot of things I want to tell you. I just can't find the right words."

She didn't speak. Her eyes were still on the blood-dotted tissue. She felt his dark eyes on her, searching, studying, assessing her.

"If I'd...known about your past..." he tried again.

Her head came up. Her eyes were as dead as stone. "You just didn't like me. It's all right. I didn't like you, either. And you couldn't have known. I came here to hide the past, not to talk about it. But I guess you were right about secrets. I'll have to find another place to go, that's all.''

He cursed under his breath. "Don't go! You're safe in Jacobsville," he continued, his voice growing stronger and more confident as he spoke. "There won't be any more suspicious reporters, no more movie deals, no more persecution. I can make sure that nobody touches you as long as you're here. I can't...protect you anywhere else," he added impatiently.

Oh, that was just great, she thought furiously. Pity. Guilt. Shame. Now he was going to go to the opposite extreme. He was going to watch over her like a protective father wolf. Well, he could think again. She scooped up one of her crutches and slammed the tip on the floor. "I don't need protection from you or anybody else. I'm leaving on the morning bus. And as for you, Mr. Caldwell, you can get out of here and leave me alone!" she raged at him.

It was the first spark of resistance he'd seen in her since he arrived. The explosion lightened his mood. She wasn't acting like a victim anymore. That was real independence in her tone, in the whole look of her. She was healing already with the retelling of that painful episode in her life.

The hesitation in him was suddenly gone. So was the somber face. Both eyebrows went up and a faint light touched his black eyes. "Or what?"

She hesitated. "What do you mean, or what?"

"If I don't get out, what do you plan to do?" he asked pleasantly.

She thought about that for a minute. "Call Ed."

He glanced at his watch. "Karla's bringing him coffee about now. Wouldn't it be a shame to spoil his break?"

She moved restlessly in the chair, still holding on to the crutch.

He smiled slowly, for the first time since he'd arrived. "Nothing more to say? Have you run out of threats already?"

Her eyes narrowed with bad temper. She didn't know what to say, or what to do. This was completely unexpected.

He studied the look of her in the pretty blue-patterned housedress she was wearing, barefoot. She was pretty, too. "I like that dress. I like your hair that color, too."

She looked at him as if she feared for his sanity. Something suddenly occurred to her. "If you didn't come rushing over here to put me on the bus and see that I left town, why are you here?"

He nodded slowly. "I was wondering when you'd get around to that." He leaned forward, just as another car pulled up outside the house.

"Ed," she guessed.

He grimaced. "I guess he rushed over to save you," he said with resignation.

She glared at him. "He was worried about me."

He went toward the door. "He wasn't the only one," he muttered, almost to himself. He opened the door before Ed could knock. "She's all in one piece," he assured his cousin, standing aside to let him into the room.

Ed was worried, confused, and obviously puzzled when he saw that she wasn't crying. "Are you all right?" he asked her.

She nodded.

Ed looked at her and then at Matt, curious, but too polite to start asking questions.

"I assume that you're staying in town now?" Matt asked her a little stiffly. "You still have a job, if you want it. No pressure. It's your decision."

She wasn't sure what to do next. She didn't want to leave Jacobsville for another town of strange people.

"Stay," Ed said gently.

She forced a smile. "I guess I could," she began. "For a while."

Matt didn't let his relief show. In a way he was glad Ed had shown up to save him from what he was about to say to her.

"You won't regret it," Ed promised her, and she smiled at him warmly.

The smile set Matt off again. He was jealous, and furious that he *was* jealous. He ran a hand through his hair again and glowered with frustration at both of them. "Oh, hell, I'm going back to work," he said shortly. "When you people get through playing games on my time, you might go to the office and earn your damned paychecks!''

He went out the door still muttering to himself, slammed into the Jaguar, and roared away.

Ed and Leslie stared at each other.

"He went to see my mother," she told him.

"And?"

"He didn't say a lot, except…except that there won't be any more reporters asking questions."

"What about Carolyn?" he asked.

"He didn't say a word about her," she murmured, having just remembered that Ed said Carolyn had gone to Houston with him. She grimaced. "I guess she'll rush home and tell the whole town about me."

"I wouldn't like to see what Matt would do about it, if she did. If he asked you to stay, it's because he plans to protect you."

"I suppose he does, but it's a shock, considering the way he was before he went out of town. Honestly, I don't know what's going on. He's like a stranger!"

"I've never heard him actually apologize," he said. "But he usually finds ways to get his point across, without saying the words."

"Maybe that was what he was doing," she replied, thinking back over his odd behavior. "He doesn't want me to leave town."

"That seems to be the case." He smiled at her. "How about it? You've still got a job if you want it, and Matt's taken you off the endangered list. You're safe here. Want to stay?''

She thought about that for a minute, about Matt's odd statement that she was safe in Jacobsville and she wouldn't be hounded anymore. It was like a dream come true after six years of running and hiding. She nodded slowly. ''Oh, yes,'' she said earnestly. ''Yes, I want to stay!''

''Then I suggest you put on your shoes and grab a jacket, and I'll drive you back to work, while we still have jobs.''

''I can't go to work like this,'' she protested.

''Why not?'' he wanted to know.

''It isn't a proper dress to wear on the job,'' she said, rising.

He scowled. ''Did Matt say that?''

''I'm not giving him the chance to,'' she said. ''From now on, I'm going to be the soul of conservatism at work. He won't get any excuses to take potshots at me.''

''If you say so,'' he said with a regretful thought for the pretty, feminine dress that he'd never seen her wear in public. So much for hoping that Matt might have coaxed her out of her repressive way of dressing. But it was early days yet.

Chapter Ten

For the first few days after her return to work, Leslie was uneasy every time she saw Matt coming. She shared that apprehension with two of the other secretaries, one of whom actually ripped her skirt climbing over the fence around the flower garden near the front of the building in a desperate attempt to escape him.

The incident sent Leslie into gales of helpless laughter as she told Karla Smith about it. Matt came by her office just as they were discussing it and stood transfixed at a sound he'd never heard coming from Leslie since he'd known her. She looked up and saw him, and made a valiant attempt to stop laughing.

''What's so funny?'' he asked pleasantly.

Karla choked and ran for the ladies' room, leaving Leslie to cope with the question.

"Did you say something to the secretaries the other day to upset them?" she asked him right out.

He shifted. "I may have said a word or two that I shouldn't have," was all he'd admit.

"Well, Daisy Joiner just plowed through a fence avoiding you, and half her petticoat's still...out... there!" She collapsed against her desk, tears rolling down her cheeks.

She was more animated than he'd ever seen her. It lifted his heart. Not that he was going to admit it.

He gave her a harsh mock glare and pulled a cigar case out of his shirt pocket. "Lily-livered cowards," he muttered as he took out a cigar, flicked off the end with a tool from his slacks pocket, and snapped open his lighter with a flair. "What we need around here are secretaries with guts!" he said loudly, and flicked the lighter with his thumb.

Two streams of water hit the flame at the same time from different directions.

"Oh, for God's sake!" Matt roared as giggling, scurrying feet retreated down the hall.

"What were you saying about secretaries with guts?" she asked with twinkling gray eyes.

He looked at his drenched lighter and his damp cigar, and threw the whole mess into the trash can by Leslie's desk. "I quit," he muttered.

Leslie couldn't help the twinkle in her eyes. "I

believe that was the whole object of the thing,'' she pointed out, "to make you quit smoking?''

He grimaced. "I guess it was.'' He studied her intently. "You're settling back in nicely,'' he remarked. "Do you have everything you need?''

"Yes,'' she replied.

He hesitated, as if he wanted to say something else and couldn't decide what. His dark eyes swept over her face, as if he were comparing her dark hair and glasses to the blond camouflage she'd worn when she first came to work for him.

"I guess I look different,'' she said a little self-consciously, because the scrutiny made her nervous. His face gave nothing away.

He smiled gently. "I like it,'' he told her.

"Did you need to see Ed?'' she asked, because he still hadn't said why he was in Ed's office.

He shrugged. "It's nothing urgent,'' he murmured. "I met with the planning and zoning committee last night. I thought he might like to know how I came out.''

"I could buzz him.''

He nodded, still smiling. "Why don't you do that?''

She did. Ed came out of his office at once, still uncertain about Matt's reactions.

"Got a minute?'' Matt asked him.

"Sure. Come on in.'' Ed stood aside to let the taller man stride into his office. He glanced back toward Leslie with a puzzled, questioning expression. She only smiled.

He nodded and closed the door, leaving Leslie to go back to work. She couldn't quite figure out Matt's new attitude toward her. There was nothing predatory about him lately. Ever since his return from Houston and the explosive meeting at her apartment, he was friendly and polite, even a little affectionate, but he didn't come near her now. He seemed to have the idea that any physical contact upset her, so he was being Big Brother Matt instead.

She should have been grateful. After all, he'd said often enough that marriage wasn't in his vocabulary. An affair, obviously, was out of the question now that he knew her past. Presumably affection was the only thing he had to offer her. It was a little disappointing, because Leslie had learned in their one early encounter that Matt's touch was delightful. She wished that she could tell him how exciting it was to her. It had been the only tenderness she'd ever had from a man in any physical respect, and she was very curious about that part of relationships. Not with just anyone, of course.

Only with Matt.

Her hands stilled on the keyboard as she heard footsteps approaching. The door opened and Carolyn came in, svelte in a beige dress that made the most of her figure, her hair perfectly coiffed.

"They said he let you come back to work here. I couldn't believe it, after what that reporter told him,"

the older woman began hotly. She gave Leslie a
haughty, contemptuous stare. "That disguise won't
do you any good, you know," she added, pausing to
dig in her purse. She drew out a worn page from an
old tabloid and tossed it onto Leslie's desk. It was
the photo they'd used of her on the stretcher, with
the caption, Teenager, Lover, Shot By Jealous
Mother In Love Triangle.

Leslie just sat and looked at it, thinking how the
past never really went away. She sighed wistfully.
She was never going to be free of it.

"Don't you have anything to say?" Carolyn
taunted.

Leslie looked up at her. "My mother is in prison.
My life was destroyed. The man responsible for it all
was a drug dealer." She searched Carolyn's cold
eyes. "You can't imagine it, can you? You've always been wealthy, protected, safe. How could you
understand the trauma of being a very innocent seventeen-year-old and having four grown men strip you
naked in a drug-crazed frenzy and try to rape you in
your own home?"

Amazingly Carolyn went pale. She hesitated,
frowning. Her eyes went to the tabloid and she
shifted uneasily. Her hand went out to retrieve the
page just as the door to Ed's office opened and Matt
came through it.

His face, when he saw Carolyn with the tearsheet
in her hand, became dangerous.

Carolyn jerked it back, crumpled it, and threw it

in the trash can. "You don't need to say anything," she said in a choked tone. "I'm not very proud of myself right now." She moved away from Leslie without looking at her. "I'm going to Europe for a few months. See you when I get back, Matt."

"You'd better hope you don't," he said in a voice like steel.

She made an awkward movement, but she didn't turn. She squared her shoulders and kept walking.

Matt paused beside the desk, retrieved the page and handed it to Ed. "Burn that," he said tautly.

"With pleasure," Ed replied. He gave Leslie a sympathetic glance before he went back into his office and closed the door.

"I thought she came to make trouble," she told Matt with evident surprise in her expression. Carolyn's abrupt about-face had puzzled her.

"She only knew what I mumbled the night I got drunk," he said curtly. "I never meant to tell her the rest of it. She's not as bad as she seems," he added. "I've known her most of my life, and I like her. She got it into her head that we should get married and saw you as a rival. I straightened all that out. At least, I thought I had."

"Thanks."

"She'll come back a different woman," he continued. "I'm sure she'll apologize."

"It's not necessary," she said. "Nobody knew the true story. I was too afraid to tell it."

He stuck his hands into his pockets and studied

her. His face was lined, his eyes had dark circles under them. He looked worn. "I would have spared you this if I could have," he gritted.

He seemed really upset about it. "You can't stop other people from thinking what they like. It's all right. I'll just have to get used to it."

"Like hell you will. The next person who comes in here with a damned tabloid page is going out right through the window!"

She smiled faintly. "Thank you. But it's not necessary. I can take care of myself."

"Judging by Carolyn's face, you did a fair job of it with her," he mused.

"I guess she's not really so bad." She glanced at him and away. "She was only jealous. It was silly. You never had designs on me."

There was a tense silence. "And what makes you think so?"

"I'm not in her league," she said simply. "She's beautiful and rich and comes from a good family."

He moved a step closer, watching her face lift. She didn't look apprehensive, so he moved again. "Not frightened?" he murmured.

"Of you?" She smiled gently. "Of course not."

He seemed surprised, curious, even puzzled.

"In fact, I like bears," she said with a deliberate grin.

That expression went right through him. He smiled. He beamed. Suddenly he caught the back of her chair with his hand and swiveled her around so that her face was within an inch of his.

"Sticks and stones, Miss Murry," he whispered softly, with a lazy grin, and brought his lips down very softly on hers.

She caught her breath.

His head lifted and his dark, quiet eyes met hers and held them while he tried to decide whether or not she was frightened. He saw the pulse throbbing at her neck and heard the faint unsteadiness of her breath. She was unsettled. But that wasn't fear. He knew enough about women to be sure of it.

He chuckled softly, and there was pure calculation in the way he studied her. "Any more smart remarks?" he taunted in a sensual whisper.

She hesitated. He wasn't aggressive or demanding or mocking. She searched his eyes, looking for clues to this new, odd behavior.

He traced her mouth with his forefinger. "Well?"

She smiled hesitantly. All her uncertainties were obvious, but she wasn't afraid of him. Her heart was going wild. But it wasn't with fear. And he knew it.

He bent and kissed her again with subdued tenderness.

"You taste like cigar smoke," she whispered impishly.

"I probably do, but I'm not giving up cigars completely, regardless of the water pistols," he whispered. "So you might as well get used to the taste of them."

She searched his dark eyes with quiet curiosity.

He put his thumb over her soft lips and smiled down at her. "I've been invited to a party at the Ballengers' next month. You'll be out of your cast by then. How about buying a pretty dress and coming with me?" He bent and brushed his lips over her forehead. "They're having a live Latin band. We can dance some more."

She wasn't hearing him. His lips were making her heart beat faster. She was smiling as she lifted her face to those soft kisses, like a flower reaching up to the sun. He realized that and smiled against her cheek.

"This isn't businesslike," she whispered.

He lifted his head and looked around. The office was empty and nobody was walking down the hall. He glanced back down at her with one lifted eyebrow.

She laughed shyly.

The teasing light in his eyes went into eclipse at the response that smile provoked in him. He framed her soft face in his big hands and bent again. This time the kiss wasn't light, or brief.

When she moaned, he drew back at once. His eyes were glittery with strong emotion. He let go of her face and stood up, looking down at her solemnly. He winced, as if he remembered previous encounters when he hadn't been careful with her, when he'd been deliberately cruel.

She read the guilt in his face and frowned. She

was totally unversed in the byplay between men and women, well past the years when those things were learned in a normal way.

"I didn't mean to do that," he said quietly. "I'm sorry."

"It's all right," she stammered.

He drew in a long, slow breath. "You have nothing to be afraid of now. I hope you know that."

"I'm not frightened," she replied.

His face hardened as he looked at her. One hand clenched in his pocket. The other clenched at his side. She happened to look down and she drew in her breath at the sight of it.

"You're hurt!" she exclaimed, reaching out to touch the abrasions that had crusted over, along with the swollen bruises that still remained there.

"I'll heal," he said curtly. "Maybe he will, too, eventually."

"He?" she queried.

"Yes. That yellow-backed reporter who came down here looking for you." His face tautened. "I took Houston apart looking for him. When I finally found him, I delivered him to his boss. There won't be any more problems from that direction, ever. In fact, he'll be writing obituaries for the rest of his miserable life."

"He could take you to court…"

"He's welcome, after my attorneys get through with him," he returned flatly. "He'll be answering charges until he's an old man. Considering the dif-

ference in our ages, I'll probably be dead by then.''
He paused to think about that. ''I'll make sure the
money's left in my estate to keep him in court until
every penny runs out!'' he added after a minute. ''He
won't even be safe when I'm six feet under!''

She didn't know whether to laugh or cry. He was
livid, almost vibrating with temper.

''But you know what hurts the most?'' he added,
looking down into her worried eyes. ''What he did
still wasn't as bad as what I did to you. I won't ever
forgive myself for that. Not if I live to be a hundred.''

That was surprising. She toyed with her keyboard
and didn't look at him. ''I thought…you might
blame me, when you knew the whole story,'' she
said.

''For what?'' he asked huskily.

She moved her shoulders restlessly. ''The papers
said it was my fault, that I invited it.''

''Dear God!'' He knelt beside her and made her
look at him. ''Your mother told me the whole story,''
he said. ''She cried like a baby when she got it all
out.'' He paused, touching her face gently. ''Know
what she said? That she'd gladly spend the rest of
her life where she is, if you could only forgive her
for what she did to you.''

She felt the tears overflowing. She started to wipe
them, but he pulled her face to his and kissed them
away so tenderly that they came in a veritable flood.

''No,'' he whispered. ''You mustn't cry. It's all

right. I won't let anything hurt you ever again. I promise.''

But she couldn't stop. ''Oh, Matt…!'' she sobbed.

All his protective instincts bristled. ''Come here to me,'' he said gently. He stood up and lifted her into his arms, cast and all, and carried her down the deserted hall to his office.

His secretary saw him coming and opened the door for him, grimacing at Leslie's red, wet face.

''Coffee or brandy?'' she asked Matt.

''Coffee. Make it about thirty minutes, will you? And hold my calls.''

''Yes, sir.''

She closed the door and Matt sat down on the burgundy couch with Leslie in his lap, cradling her while she wept.

He tucked a handkerchief into her hand and rocked her in his arms, whispering to her until the sobs lessened.

''I'm going to replace the furniture in here,'' he murmured. ''Maybe the paneling, too.''

''Why?''

''It must hold some painful memories for you,'' he said. ''I know it does for me.''

His voice was bitter. She recalled fainting, and coming to on this very couch. She looked up at him without malice or accusation. Her eyes were red and swollen, and full of curiosity.

He traced her cheek with tender fingers and smiled at her. ''You've had a rough time of it, haven't you?'' he asked quietly. ''Will it do any good to tell you that a man wouldn't normally treat a woman, especially an innocent woman, the way those animals treated you?''

''I know that,'' she replied. ''It's just that the publicity made me out to be little more than a call girl. I'm not like that. But it's what people thought I was. So I ran, and ran, and hid…if it hadn't been for Ed and his father, and my friend Jessica, I don't know what I would have done. I don't have any family left.''

''You have your mother,'' he assured her. ''She'd like to see you. If you're willing, I'll drive you up there, anytime you like.''

She hesitated. ''You do know that she's in prison for murder?'' she asked.

''I know it.''

''You're well-known here,'' she began.

''Oh, good Lord, are you trying to save me?'' he asked with an exasperated sigh. ''Woman, I don't give two hoots in hell for gossip. While they're talking about me, they're leaving some other person alone.'' He took the handkerchief and wiped her cheeks. ''But for the record, most reporters keep out of my way.'' He pursed his lips. ''I can guarantee there's one in Houston who'll run the next time he sees me coming.''

It amazed her that he'd gone to that much trouble defending her. She lay looking at him with eyes like a cat's, wide and soft and curious.

They had an odd effect on him. He felt his body react to it and caught his breath. He started to move her before she realized that he was aroused.

The abrupt rejection startled her. All at once she was sitting beside him on the couch, looking stunned.

He got up quickly and moved away, turning his back to her. "How would you like some coffee?" he asked gruffly.

She shifted a little, staring at him with open curiosity. "I...I would, thank you."

He went to the intercom, not to the door, and told his secretary to bring it in. He kept his back to Leslie, and to the door, even when Edna came in with the coffee service and placed it on the low coffee table in front of the sofa.

"Thanks, Edna," he said.

"Sure thing, boss." She winked at Leslie and smiled reassuringly, closing the door quietly behind her.

Leslie poured coffee into the cups, glancing at him warily. "Don't you want your coffee?"

"Not just yet," he murmured, trying to cool down.

"It smells nice."

"Yes, it does, but I've already had a little too much stimulation for the moment, without adding caffeine to the problem."

She didn't understand. He felt her eyes on his stiff back and with a helpless laugh, he turned around. To his amazement, and his amusement, she didn't notice anything wrong with him.

He went back to the couch and sat down, shaking his head as he let her hand him a cupful of fresh coffee.

"Is something wrong?" she asked.

"Not a thing in this world, baby doll," he drawled. "Except that Edna just saved you from absolute ruin and you don't even know it."

Leslie stared into Matt's dancing eyes with obvious confusion.

"Never mind," he chuckled, sipping his coffee. "One day when we know each other better, I'll tell you all about it."

She sipped her coffee and smiled absently. "You're very different since you came back from Houston."

"I've had a bad knock." He put his cup down, but his eyes stayed on it. "I can't remember ever being grossly unfair to anyone before, much less an employee. It's hard for me, remembering some of the things I said and did to you." He grimaced, still not looking straight at her. "It hurt my pride that you'd let Ed get close, but you kept backing away from me. I never stopped to wonder why." He laughed hollowly. "I've had women throw themselves at me most of my adult life, even before I made my first million." He glanced at her. "But I couldn't get near you, except once, on the dance floor." His eyes narrowed. "And that night, when you let me touch you."

She remembered, too, the feel of his eyes and his

hands and his mouth on her. Her breath caught audibly.

He winced. "It was the first time, wasn't it?"

She averted her eyes.

"I even managed to soil that one, beautiful memory." He looked down at his hands. "I've done so much damage, Leslie. I don't know how to start over, to begin again."

"Neither do I," she confessed. "What happened to me in Houston was a pretty bad experience, even if I'd been older and more mature when it happened. As it was, I gave up trying to go on dates afterward, because I connected anything physical with that one sordid incident. I couldn't bear it when men wanted to kiss me good-night. I backed away and they thought I was some sort of freak." Her eyes closed and she shuddered.

"Tell me about the doctor."

She hesitated. "He only knew what he'd been told, I guess. But he made me feel like trash." She wrapped both arms around her chest and leaned forward. "He cleaned the wound and bandaged my leg. He said that they could send me back to the hospital from jail for the rest."

Matt muttered something vicious.

"I didn't go to jail, of course, my mother did. The leg was horribly painful. I had no medical insurance and Jessica's parents were simple people, very poor. None of us could have afforded orthopedic surgery. I was able to see a doctor at the local clinic, and he put a cast on it, assuming that it had already been set properly. He didn't do X rays because I couldn't afford any.''

''You're lucky the damage could even be repaired,'' he said, his eyes downcast as he wondered at the bad luck she'd had not only with the trauma of the incident itself, but with its painful aftermath.

''I had a limp when it healed, but I walked fairly well.'' She sighed. ''Then I fell off a horse.'' She shook her head.

''I wouldn't have had that happen for the world,'' he said, meeting her eyes. ''I was furious, not just that you'd backed away from me, but that I'd caused you to hurt yourself. Then at the dance, it was even worse, when I realized that all those quick steps had caused you such pain.''

''It was a good sort of pain,'' she told him, ''because it led to corrective surgery. I'm really grateful about that.''

''I'm sorry it came about in the way it did.'' He smiled at her new look. ''Glasses suit you. They make your eyes look bigger.''

''I always wore them until the reporter started trying to sell an idea for a television movie about what happened. I dyed my hair and got contacts, dressed like a dowager, did everything I could to change my appearance. But Jacobsville was my last chance. I thought if I could be found here, I could be tracked anywhere.'' She smoothed her skirt over the cast.

''You won't be bothered by that anymore,'' he

said. "But I'd like to let my attorneys talk to your mother. I know," he said, when she lifted her head and gave him a worried look, "it would mean resurrecting a lot of unpleasant memories, but we might be able to get her sentence reduced or even get her a new trial. There were extenuating circumstances. Even a good public defender isn't as good as an experienced criminal lawyer."

"Did you ask her that?"

He nodded. "She wouldn't even discuss it. She said you'd had enough grief because of her."

She lowered her eyes back to her skirt. "Maybe we both have. But I hate it that she may spend the rest of her life in prison."

"So do I." He touched her hair. "She really is blond, isn't she?"

"Yes. My father had dark hair, like mine, and gray eyes, too. Hers are blue. I always wished mine were that color."

"I like your eyes just the way they are." He touched the wire rims of her frames. "Glasses and all."

"You don't have any problem seeing, do you?" she wondered.

He chuckled. "I have trouble seeing what's right under my nose, apparently."

"You're farsighted?" she asked, misunderstanding him.

He touched her soft mouth with his forefinger and the smile faded. "No. I mistake gold for tinsel."

His finger made her feel nervous. She drew back. His hand fell at once and he smiled at her surprise.

"No more aggression. I promise."

Her fascinated eyes met his. "Does that mean that you won't ever kiss me again?" she asked boldly.

"Oh, I will," he replied, delighted. He leaned forward. "But you'll have to do all the chasing from now on."

Chapter Eleven

Leslie searched his dark eyes slowly and then she began to smile. "Me, chase you?" she asked.

He pursed his lips. "Sure. Men get tired of the chase from time to time. I think I'd like having you pursue me."

Mental pictures of her in a suit and Matt in a dress dissolved her in mirth. But the reversed relationship made her feel warm inside, as if she wasn't completely encased in ice. The prospect of Matt in her arms was exhilarating, even with her past. "Okay, but I draw the line at taking you to football games," she added, trying to keep things casual between them, just for the time being.

He grinned back. "No problem. We can always

watch them on TV.'' The light in her eyes made him light-headed. ''Feeling better now?'' he asked softly.

She nodded. ''I guess you can get used to anything when you have to,'' she said philosophically.

''I could write you a book on that,'' he said bitterly, and she remembered his past—his young life marked with such sadness.

''I'm sure you could,'' she agreed.

He leaned forward with the coffee cup still in his hands. He had nice hands, she thought absently, lean and strong and beautifully shaped. She remembered their touch on her body with delight.

''We'll take this whole thing one step at a time,'' he said quietly. ''There won't be any pressure, and I won't run roughshod over you. We'll go at your pace.''

She was a little reluctant. That one step at a time could lead anywhere, and she didn't like the idea of taking chances. He wasn't a marrying man and she wasn't the type for affairs. She did wonder what he ultimately had in mind for them, but she wasn't confident enough of this new relationship to ask. It was nice to have him like this, gentle and concerned and caring. She hadn't had much tenderness in her life, and she was greedy for it.

He glanced suddenly at the thin gold watch on his wrist and grimaced. ''I should have been in Fort Worth an hour ago for a meeting with some stock producers.'' He glanced at her ruefully. ''Just look at what you do to me," he murmured. "I can't even think straight anymore."

She smiled gently. "Good for me."

He chuckled, finished his coffee and put down the cup. "Better late than never, I suppose." He leaned down and kissed her, very softly. His eyes held a new, warm light that made her feel funny all over. "Stay out of trouble while I'm gone."

Her eyebrows rose. "Oh, that's cute."

He nodded. "You never put a foot wrong, did you?"

"Only by being stupid and gullible."

His dark eyes went even darker. "What happened wasn't your fault. That's the first idea we have to correct."

"I was madly infatuated for the first time in my life," she said honestly. "I might have inadvertently given him the idea...."

He put his thumb against her soft lips. "Leslie, what sort of decent adult man would accept even blatant signals from a teenager?"

It was a good question. It made her see what had happened from a different perspective.

He gave her mouth a long scrutiny before he abruptly removed his thumb and ruffled her short dark hair playfully. "Think about that. You might also consider that people on drugs very often don't know what they're doing anyway. You were in the wrong place at the wrong time."

She readjusted her glasses as they slipped further on her nose. "I suppose so."

"I'll be in Fort Worth overnight, but maybe we can go out to dinner tomorrow night?" he asked speculatively.

She indicated the cast. "I can see me now, clumping around in a pretty dress."

He chuckled. "I don't mind if you don't."

She'd never been on a real date before, except nights out with Ed, who was more like a brother than a boyfriend. Her eyes brightened. "I'd love to go out with you, if you mean it."

"I mean it, all right."

"Then, yes."

He grinned at her. "Okay."

She couldn't look away from his dark, soft eyes. It felt like electricity flowing between them. It was exciting to share that sort of intimate look. She colored. He arched an eyebrow and gave her a wicked smile.

"Not now," he said in a deep, husky tone that made her blush even more, and turned toward the door.

He opened it. "Edna, I'll be back tomorrow," he told his secretary.

"Yes, sir."

He didn't look back. The outer door opened and closed. Leslie got up with an effort and moved to the office door. "Do you want me to clean up in here?" she asked Edna.

The older woman just smiled. "Heavens, no. You go on back to work, Miss Murry. How's that leg feeling?"

"Awkward," she said, glowering at it. "But it's going to be nice not to limp anymore," she added truthfully. "I'm very grateful to Mr. Caldwell for having it seen to."

"He's a good man," his secretary said with a smile. "And a good boss. He has moods, but most people do."

"Yes."

Leslie clumped her way back down the hall to her office. Ed came out when he heard her rustling paper and lifted both eyebrows. "Feeling better?" he asked.

She nodded. "I'm a watering pot lately. I don't know why."

"Nobody ever had a better reason," he ventured. He smiled gently. "Matt's not so bad, is he?"

She shook her head. "He's not what I thought he was at first."

"He'll grow on you," he said. He reached for a file on his desk, brought it out and perched himself on the edge of her desk. "I need you to answer these. Feel up to some dictation?"

She nodded. "You bet!"

Matt came back late the next morning and went straight to Leslie when he arrived at the office. "Call Karla Smith and ask if she'll substitute for you," he said abruptly. "You and I are going to take the afternoon off."

"We are?" she asked, pleasantly surprised. "What are we going to do?"

"Now there's a leading question," he said, chuckling. He pressed the intercom on her phone and told Ed he was swiping his secretary and then moved back while Leslie got Karla on the phone and asked her to come down to Ed's office.

It didn't take much time to arrange everything. Minutes later, she was seated beside Matt in the Jaguar flying down the highway just at the legal speed limit.

"Where are we going?" she asked excitedly.

He grinned, glancing sideways at the picture she made in that pretty blue-and-green swirl-patterned dress that left her arms bare. He liked her hair short and dark. He even liked her glasses.

"I've got a surprise for you," he said. "I hope you're going to like it," he added a little tautly.

"Don't tell me. You're taking me to see all the big snakes at the zoo," she said jokingly.

"Do you like snakes?" he asked unexpectedly.

"Not really. But that would be a surprise I wouldn't quite like," she added.

"No snakes."

"Good."

He slid into the passing lane and passed several other cars on the four-lane.

"This is the road to Houston," she said, noting a road sign.

"So it is."

She toyed with her seat belt. "Matt, I don't really like Houston."

"I know that." He glanced at her. "We're going to the prison to see your mother."

Her intake of breath was audible. Her hands clenched on her skirt.

He reached a lean hand over and gently pressed both of hers. "Remember what Ed says? Never back away from a problem," he said softly. "Always meet it head-on. You and your mother haven't seen each other in over five years. Don't you think it's time to lay rest to all the ghosts?"

She was uneasy and couldn't hide it. "The last time I saw her was in court, when the verdict was read. She wouldn't even look at me."

"She was ashamed, Leslie."

That was surprising. Her eyes met his under a frown. "Ashamed?"

"She wasn't taking huge amounts of drugs, but she was certainly addicted. She'd had something before she went back to the apartment and found you with her lover. The drugs disoriented her. She told me that she doesn't even remember how the pistol got into her hand, the next thing she knew, her lover was dead and you were bleeding on the floor. She barely remembers the police taking her away." His lips flattened. "What she does remember is coming back to her senses in jail and being told what she did. No, she didn't look at you during the trial or afterward. It wasn't that she blamed you. She blamed herself for being so gullible and letting herself be taken in by a smooth-talking, lying drug dealer who pretended to love her in return for a place to live.''

She didn't like the memories. She and her mother had never been really close, but when she looked back, she remembered that she'd been standoffish and difficult, especially after the death of her father.

His hand contracted on both of hers. ''I'm going to be right with you every step of the way,'' he said firmly. ''Whatever happens, it won't make any difference to me. I only want to try to make things easier for you.''

''She might not want to see me,'' she ventured.

''She wants to,'' he said grimly. ''Very badly. She realizes that she might not have much time left.''

She bit her lower lip. ''I never realized she had heart trouble.''

''She probably didn't, until she started consuming massive quantities of drugs. The human body can only take so much abuse until it starts rebelling.'' He glanced at her. ''She's all right for now. She just has to take it easy. But I still think we can do something for her.''

''A new trial would put a lot of stress on her.''

''It would,'' he agreed. ''But perhaps it isn't the sort of stress that would be damaging. At the end of that road, God willing, she might get out on parole.''

Leslie only nodded. The difficult part lay yet ahead of her; a reunion that she wasn't even sure she wanted. But Matt seemed determined to bring it about.

It was complicated to get into a prison, Leslie learned at once. There were all sorts of checkpoints and safety measures designed to protect visitors. Leslie shivered a little as they walked down the long hall to the room where visitors were allowed to see inmates. For her, the thought of losing her freedom was akin to fears of a lingering death. She wondered if it was that bad for her mother.

There was a long row of chairs at little cubicles, separated from the prisoners' side by thick glass. There was a small opening in the glass, which was covered with mesh wiring so that people could talk back and forth. Matt spoke to a guard and gestured Leslie toward one of the cubicles, settling her in the straight-backed chair there. Through the glass, she could see a closed door across the long room.

As she watched, aware of Matt's strong, warm hand on her shoulder, the door opened and a thin, drawn blond woman with very short hair was ushered into the room by a guard. She went forward to the cubicle where Leslie was sitting and lifted her eyes to the tense face through the glass. Her pale blue eyes were full of sadness and uncertainty. Her thin hands trembled.

"Hello, Leslie," she said slowly.

Leslie just sat there for a moment with her heart beating half to death. The thin, drawn woman with the heavily lined face and dull blue eyes was only a shadow of the mother she remembered. Those thin hands were so wasted that the blue veins on their backs stood out prominently.

Marie smiled with faint self-contempt. "I knew this would be a mistake," she said huskily. "I'm so sorry…" She started to get up.

"Wait," Leslie croaked. She grimaced. She didn't know what to say. The years had made this woman a stranger.

Matt moved behind her, both hands on her shoulders now, supporting her, giving her strength.

"Take your time," he said gently. "It's all right."

Marie gave a little start as she noticed that Matt was touching Leslie with some familiarity, and Leslie wasn't stiff or protesting. Her eyes connected with his dark ones and he smiled.

Marie smiled back hesitantly. It changed her lined, worn face and made her seem younger. She looked into her daughter's eyes and her own softened. "I like your boss," she said.

Leslie smiled back. "I like him, too," she confessed.

There was a hesitation. "I don't know where to start," she began huskily. "I've rehearsed it and rehearsed it and I simply can't find the words." Her pale eyes searched Leslie's face, as if she was trying to recall it from the past. She winced as she compared it with the terror-stricken face she'd seen that night so long ago. "I've made a lot of mistakes, Leslie. My biggest one was putting my own needs ahead of everybody else's. It was always what *I* wanted, what *I* needed. Even when I started doing drugs, all I thought about was what would make me happy." She shook her head. "Selfishness carries a high price tag. I'm so sorry that you had to pay such a high price for mine. I couldn't even bear to look at you at the trial, after the tabloids came out. I was so ashamed of what I'd subjected you to. I thought of you, all alone, trying to hold your head up with half the state knowing such intimate things about our lives…" She drew in a slow, unsteady breath and she seemed to slump. "I can't even ask you to forgive me. But I did want to see you, even if it's just this once, to tell you how much I regret it all."

The sight of her pinched face hurt Leslie, who hadn't realized her mother even felt remorse. There had been no communication between them. She knew now that Matt had been telling the truth about her mother's silence. Marie was too ashamed to face her, even now. It eased the wound a little. "I didn't know about the drugs," Leslie blurted out abruptly.

Her tone brought Marie's eyes up, and for the first time, there was hope in them. "I never used them around you," she said gently. "But it started a long time ago, about the time your father…died." The light in her eyes seemed to dim. "You blamed me for his death, and you were right. He couldn't live up to being what I wanted him to be. He couldn't give me the things I thought I deserved.'' She looked down at the table in front of her. ''He was a good, kind man. I should have appreciated him. It wasn't until he died that I realized how much he meant to me. And it was too late.'' She laughed hollowly. ''From then on, everything went downhill. I didn't care anymore, about myself or you, and I went onto harder drugs. That's how I met Mike. I guess you figured out that he was my supplier.''

''Matt did,'' Leslie corrected.

Marie lifted her eyes to look at Matt, who was still standing behind Leslie. ''Don't let them hurt her anymore,'' she pleaded gently. ''Don't let that reporter make her run anymore. She's had enough.''

''So have you,'' Leslie said unexpectedly, painfully touched by Marie's concern. ''Matt says…that he thinks his attorneys might be able to get you a new trial.''

Marie started. Her eyes lit up, and then abruptly shifted. ''No!'' she said gruffly. ''I have to pay for what I did.''

''Yes,'' Leslie said. ''But what you did…'' She hesitated. ''What you did was out of shock and outrage, don't you see? It wasn't premeditated. I don't know much about the law, but I do know that intent is everything. You didn't plan to kill Mike.''

The older woman's sad eyes met Leslie's through the glass. ''That's generous of you, Leslie,'' she said quietly. ''Very generous, considering the notoriety and grief I caused you.''

''We've both paid a price,'' she agreed.

''You're wearing a cast,'' her mother said suddenly. ''Why?''

''I fell off a horse,'' Leslie said and felt Matt's hands contract on her shoulders, as if he was remembering why. She reached up and smoothed her hand over one of his. ''It was a lucky fall, because Matt got an orthopedic surgeon to operate on my leg and put it right.''

''Do you know how her leg was hurt?'' the other woman asked Matt with a sad little smile.

''Yes,'' he replied. His voice sounded strained. The tender, caressing action of Leslie's soft fingers on his hand was arousing him. It was the first time she'd touched him voluntarily, and his head was reeling.

''That's another thing I've had on my conscience for years,'' the smaller woman told her daughter. ''I'm glad you had the operation.''

''I'm sorry for the position you're in,'' Leslie said with genuine sympathy. ''I would have come to see you years ago, but I thought…I thought you hated me,'' she added huskily, ''for what happened to Mike.''

''Oh, Leslie!'' Marie put her face in her hands and her shoulders shook. She wept harshly, while her daughter sat staring at her uncomfortably. After a minute, she wiped the tears from her red, swollen eyes. "No, I didn't hate you! I never blamed you!" Marie said brokenly. "How could I hate you for something that was never your fault? I wasn't a good mother. I put you at risk the minute I started using drugs. I failed you terribly. By letting Mike move in, I set you up for what he and his friends did to you. My poor baby," she choked. "You were so very young, so innocent, and to have men treat you…that way—" She broke off. "That's why I couldn't ask you to come, why I couldn't write or phone. I thought you hated *me!*"

Leslie's fingers clenched around Matt's on her shoulder, drawing strength from his very presence. She knew she could never have faced this without him. "I didn't hate you," she said slowly. "I'm sorry we couldn't talk to each other, at the trial. I…did blame you for Dad," she confessed. "But I was so young when it happened, and you and I had never been particularly close. If we had…"

"You can't change what was," her mother said with a wistful smile. "But it's worth all this if you can forgive me." Her long fingers moved restlessly on the receiver. Her pained eyes met Leslie's. "It means everything if you can forgive me!"

Leslie felt a lump in her throat as she looked at her mother and realized the change in her. "Of course I can." She bit her lip. "Are you all right? Is your health all right?"

"I have a weak heart, probably damaged by all the drugs I took," Marie said without emphasis. "I take medicine for it, and I'm doing fine. I'll be all right, Leslie." She searched the younger woman's eyes intently. "I hope you're going to be all right, too, now that you aren't being stalked by that reporter anymore. Thank you for coming to see me."

"I'm glad I did," Leslie said, and meant it sincerely. "I'll write, and I'll come to see you when I can. Meanwhile, Matt's lawyers may be able to do something for you. Let them try."

There was a hesitation while the other woman exchanged a worried look with Matt.

Both his hands pressed on Leslie's shoulders. "I'll take care of her," he told Marie, and knew that she understood what he was saying. Nobody would bother Leslie again, as long as there was a breath in his body. He had power and he would use it on her daughter's behalf. She relaxed.

"All right, then," she replied. "Thank you for trying to help me, even if nothing comes of it."

Matt smiled at her. "Miracles happen every day," he said, and he was looking at Leslie's small hand caressing his.

"You hold on to him," the older woman told Leslie fervently. "If I'd had a man like that to care about me, I wouldn't be in this mess today."

Leslie flushed. Her mother spoke as if she had a chance of holding on to Matt, and that was absurd.

He might feel guilt and sympathy, even regret, but her mother seemed to be mistaking his concern for love. It wasn't.

Matt leaned close to Leslie and spoke. "It's rather the other way around," Matt said surprisingly, and he didn't smile. "Women like Leslie don't grow on trees."

Marie smiled broadly. "No, they don't. She's very special. Take care of yourself, Leslie. I…I do love you, even if it doesn't seem like it."

Leslie's eyes stung with threatening tears. "I love you, too, Mama," she said in a gruff, uneasy tone. She could barely speak for the emotion she felt.

The other woman couldn't speak at all. Her eyes were bright and her smile trembled. She only nodded. After one long look at her daughter, she got up and went to the door.

Leslie sat there for a minute, watching until her mother was completely out of sight. Matt's big hands contracted on her shoulders.

"Let's go, sweetheart," he said gently, and pressed a handkerchief into her hands as he shepherded her out the door.

That tenderness in him was a lethal weapon, she thought. It was almost painful to experience, especially when she knew that it wasn't going to last. He was kind, and right now he was trying to make amends. But she'd better not go reading anything into his actions. She had to take one day at a time and just live for the present.

She was quiet all the way to the parking lot. Matt smoked a cigar on the way, one hand in his pocket, his eyes narrow and introspective as he strode along beside Leslie until they reached the car. He pushed a button on his electronic controller and the locks popped up.

"Thank you for bringing me here," Leslie said at the passenger door, her eyes full of gratitude as they lifted to his. "I'm really glad I came, even if I didn't want to at first."

He stayed her hand as she went to open the door and moved closer, so that she was standing between his long, muscular body and the door. His dark eyes searched hers intently.

His gaze fell to her soft mouth and the intensity of the look parted her lips. Her pulse raced like mad. Her reaction to his closeness had always been intense, but she could almost feel his mouth on her body as she looked up at him. It was frightening to feel such wanton impulses.

His eyes lifted and he saw that expression in her soft, dazed gray eyes. The muscles in his jaw moved and he seemed to be holding his breath.

Around them, the parking lot was deserted. There was nothing audible except the sound of traffic and the frantic throb of Leslie's pulse as she stared into Matt's dark, glittery eyes.

He moved a step closer, deliberately positioning his body so that one long, powerful leg brushed between her good leg and the bulky cast on the other one.

"Matt?" she whispered shakily.

His eyes narrowed. His free hand went to her face and spread against her flushed cheek. His thumb nudged at her chin, lifting it. His leg moved against her thighs and she gasped.

There was arrogance not only in the way he touched her, but in the way he looked at her. She was completely vulnerable when he approached her like this, and he must surely know it, with his experience of women.

"So many women put on an act," he murmured conversationally. "They pretend to be standoffish, they tease, they provoke, they exaggerate their responses. With you, it's all genuine. I can look at you and see everything you're thinking. You don't try to hide it or explain it. It's all right there in the open."

Her lips parted. It was getting very hard to breathe. She didn't know what to say.

His head bent just a little, so that she could feel his breath on her mouth. "You can't imagine the pleasure it gives me to see you like this. I feel ten feet tall."

"Why?" she whispered unsteadily.

His mouth hovered over hers, lightly brushing, teasing. "Because every time I touch you, you offer yourself up like a virgin sacrifice. I remember the taste of your breasts in my mouth, the soft little cries that pulsed out of you when I pressed you down into the mattress under my body." He moved against her, slowly and deliberately, letting her feel his instant response. "I want to take your clothes off and ease inside your body on crisp, white sheets..." he whispered as his hard mouth went down roughly on her soft lips.

She made a husky little cry as she pictured what he was saying to her, pictured it, ached for it. Of all the outrageous, shocking things to say to a woman...!

Her nails bit into his arms as she lifted herself against his arousal and pushed up at his mouth to tempt it into violence. The sudden whip of passion was unexpected, overwhelming. She moaned brokenly and her legs trembled.

He groaned harshly. For a few seconds, his mouth devoured her own. He had to drag himself away from her, and when he did, his whole body seemed to vibrate. There was a flush high on his cheekbones, and his eyes glittered.

She loved the expression on his face. She loved the tremor of the arms propped on either side of her head. Her chin lifted and her eyes grew misty with pleasure.

"Do you like making me this way?" he asked gruffly.

"Yes," she said, something wild and impulsive rising in her like a quick tide. She looked at the pulse in his throat, the quick rhythmic movement of his shirt under the suit he was wearing. Her eyes dropped boldly down his body to the visible effect of passion on him.

His intake of breath was audible as he watched her eyes linger on him, there. His whole body shook convulsively, as if with a fever.

Her eyes went back to his. It was intimate, to look at him this way. She could feel his passion, taste it.

Her hands went to his chest and rested against his warm muscles through the shirt, feeling the soft cushion of hair under it. He wasn't trying to stop her, and she remembered what he'd said to her in his office, that she was going to have to make all the running. Well, why not? She had to find out sooner or later what the limits of her capability were. Now seemed as good a time as any, despite their surroundings. Shyly, involuntarily, her nervous hands slid down to his belt and hesitated.

His jaw clenched. He was helpless. Did she know? Her hands slowly moved over the belt and down barely an inch before they hesitated again. His heavy brows drew together in a ferocious scowl as he fought for control.

He seemed to turn to stone. There was not a trace

of emotion on his lean, hard face, but his eyes were glittering wildly.

"Go ahead if you want to. But if you touch me there," he said in a choked, harsh tone, "I will back you into this car, push your skirt up, and take you right here in the parking lot without a second's hesitation. And I won't give a damn if the entire staff of the prison comes out to watch!"

Chapter Twelve

The terse threat brought Leslie to her senses. She went scarlet as her hands jerked back from his body.

"Oh, good Lord!" she said, horrified at what she'd been doing.

Matt closed his eyes and leaned his forehead against hers. It was damp with sweat and he shuddered with helpless reaction even as he laughed at her embarrassment.

She could barely get her own breath, and her body felt swollen all over. "I'm sorry, Matt, I don't know what got into me!"

The raging desire she'd kindled was getting the best of him. He'd wanted her for such a long time. He hadn't even thought of other women. "Leslie,

I'm fairly vulnerable, and you're starting something both of us know you can't finish,'' he added huskily.

"I'm...not sure that I can't,'' she said, surprising both of them. She felt the damp warmth of his body close to hers and marveled at his vulnerability.

His eyes opened. He lifted his head slowly and looked down at her, his breath on her mouth. "If you have a single instinct for self-preservation left, you'd better get in the car, Leslie.''

"Okay,'' she agreed breathlessly, her heart in her eyes as she looked at him with faint wonder.

She got in on the passenger side and fastened her seat belt. He came around to the driver's side and got into the car.

Her hands were curling in on the soft material of her purse and she looked everywhere except at him. She couldn't believe what she'd done.

"Don't make such heavy weather of it,'' he said gently. "I did say that you'd have to do the chasing, after all.''

She cleared her throat. "I think I took it a little too literally.''

He chuckled. The sound was deep and pleasant as the powerful car ate up the miles toward Jacobsville. "You have definite potential, Miss Murry,'' he mused, glancing at her with indulgent affection. "I think we're making progress.''

She stared at her purse. "Slow progress.''

"That's the best kind.'' He changed gears and passed a slow-moving old pickup truck. "I'll drop you by your house to change. We're going out on the town tonight, cast and all."

She smiled shyly. "I can't dance."

"There's plenty of time for dancing when you're back on your feet," he said firmly. "I'm going to take care of you from now on. No more risks."

He made her feel like treasure. She didn't realize she'd spoken aloud until she heard him chuckle.

"That's what you are," he said. "My treasure. I'm going to have a hard time sharing you even with other people." He glanced at her. "You're sure there's nothing between you and Ed?"

"Only friendship," she assured him.

"Good."

He turned on the radio and he looked more relaxed than she'd ever seen him. It was like a beginning. She had no idea where their relationship would go, but she was too weak to stop now.

They went out to eat, and Matt was the soul of courtesy. He opened doors for her, pulled out chairs for her, did all the little things that once denoted a gentleman and proved to her forcefully that he wasn't a completely modern man. She loved it. Old World courtesy was delicious.

They went to restaurants in Jacobsville and Victoria and Houston in the weeks that followed, and Matt even phoned her late at night, just to talk. He sent her flowers at the boardinghouse, prompting teasing remarks and secret smiles from other residents. He was Leslie's fellow, in the eyes of Jacobsville, and she began to feel as if her dreams might actually come true—except for the one problem that had never been addressed. How was she going to react when Matt finally made love to her completely? Would she be able to go through with intimacy like that, with her past?

It haunted her, because while Matt had been affectionate and kind and tender with her, it never went beyond soft, brief kisses in his car or at her door. He never attempted to take things to a deeper level, and she was too shy from their encounter at the prison parking lot to be so bold again.

The cast came off just before the Ballengers' party to which all of Jacobsville was invited. Leslie looked at her unnaturally pale leg with fascination as Lou Coltrain coaxed her into putting her weight on it for the first time without the supporting cast.

She did, worried that it wouldn't take her weight, while Matt stood grim-faced next to Lou and worried with her.

But when she felt the strength of the bone, she gasped. "It's all right!" she exclaimed. "Matt, look, I can stand on it!"

"Of course you can," Lou chuckled. "Dr. Santos is the best, the very best, in orthopedics."

"I'll be able to dance again," she said.

Matt moved forward and took her hand in his, lifting it to his mouth. *"We'll* be able to dance again," he corrected, holding her eyes with his.

Lou had to stifle amusement at the way they looked together, the tall dark rancher and the small brunette, like two halves of a whole. That would be some marriage, she thought privately, but she kept her thoughts to herself.

Later, Matt came to pick her up at her apartment. She was wearing the long silver dress with the spaghetti straps, and this time without a bra under it. She felt absolutely vampish with her contacts back in and her hair clean and shining. She'd gained a little weight in the past few weeks, and her figure was all she'd ever hoped it would be. Best of all, she could walk without limping.

"Nice," he murmured, smiling as they settled themselves into the car. "But we're not going to overdo things, are we?"

"Whatever you say, boss," she drawled.

He chuckled as he cranked the car. "That's a good start to the evening."

"I have something even better planned for later," she said demurely.

His heart jumped and his fingers jerked on the steering wheel. "Is that a threat or a promise?"

She glanced at him shyly. "That depends on you."

He didn't speak for a minute. "Leslie, you can only go so far with a man before things get out of hand," he began slowly. "You don't know much about relationships, because you haven't dated. I want you to understand how it is with me. I haven't touched another woman since I met you. That makes me more vulnerable than I would be normally." His eyes touched her profile and averted to the highway. "I can't make light love to you anymore," he said finally, his voice harsh. "The strain is more than I can bear."

Her breath caught. She smoothed at an imaginary spot on her gown. "You want us to...to go on like we are."

"I do not," he said gruffly. "But I'm not going to put any pressure on you. I meant what I said about letting you make the moves."

She turned the small purse over in her hands, watching the silver sequins on it glitter in the light. "You've been very patient."

"Because I was very careless of you in those first weeks we knew each other," he said flatly. "I'm trying to show you that sex isn't the basis of our relationship."

She smiled. "I knew that already," she replied. "You've taken wonderful care of me."

He shrugged. "Penance."

She grinned, because it wasn't. He'd shown her in a hundred nonverbal ways how he felt about her. Even the other women in the office had remarked on it.

He glanced at her. "No comment?"

"Oh, I'm sorry, I was just thinking about something."

"About what?" he asked conversationally.

She traced a sequin on the purse. "Can you teach me how to seduce you?"

The car went off the road and barely missed a ditch before he righted it, pulled onto the shoulder and flipped the key to shut off the engine.

He gaped at her. "What did you say?"

She looked up at him in the dimly lit interior where moonlight reflected into the car. "I want to seduce you."

"Maybe I have a fever," he murmured.

She smiled. She laughed. He made her feel as if she could do anything. Her whole body felt warm and uninhibited. She leaned back in her seat and moved sinuously in the seat, liking the way the silky fabric felt against her bare breasts. She felt reckless.

His gaze fell to the fabric against which her hard nipples were distinctly outlined. He watched her body move and knew that she was already aroused, which aroused him at once.

He leaned over, his mouth catching hers as his lean hand slipped under the fabric and moved lazily against her taut breasts.

She moaned and arched toward his fingers, pulling them back when he would have removed them. Her mouth opened under his as she gave in to the need to experience him in a new way, in a new intimacy.

"This is dangerous." He bit off the words against her mouth.

"It feels wonderful," she whispered back, pressing his hand to her soft skin. "I want to feel you like this. I want to touch you under your shirt..."

He hadn't realized how quickly he could get a tie and a shirt out of the way. He pulled her across the console and against him, watching her pert breasts bury themselves in the thick hair that covered his chest. He moved her deliberately against it and watched her eyes grow languid and misty as she experienced him.

His mouth opened hers in a sensual kiss that was as explicit as lovemaking. She felt his tongue, his lips, his teeth, and all the while, his chest moved lazily against her bare breasts. His hand went to the base of her spine and moved her upon the raging arousal she'd kindled. He groaned harshly, and she knew that he wouldn't draw back tonight. The strange thing, the wonderful thing, was that she wasn't afraid.

A minute later, he forced his head up and looked at her, lying yielding and breathless against him. He touched her breasts possessively before he lifted his eyes to search hers. "You aren't afraid of me like this," he said huskily.

She drew in a shaking breath. "No. I'm not."

His eyes narrowed as he persisted. "You want me."

She nodded. She touched his lips with fingers that

trembled. "I want you very much. I like the way you feel when you want me," she whispered daringly, the surprise of it in her expression as she moved restlessly against him. "It excites me to feel it."

He groaned out loud and closed his eyes. "For God's sake, honey, don't say things like that to me!"

Her fingers moved down to his chest and pressed there. "Why not? I want to know if I can be intimate with you. I have to know," she said hesitantly. "I've never been able to want a man before. And I've never felt anything like this!" She looked up into his open, curious eyes. "Matt, can we…go somewhere?" she whispered.

"And make love?" he asked in a tone that suggested he thought she was unbalanced.

Her expression softened. "Yes."

He couldn't. His brain told him he couldn't. But his stupid body was screaming at him that he certainly could! "Leslie, sweetheart, it's too soon…"

"No, it isn't," she said huskily, tracing the hair on his chest with cool fingers. "I know you don't want anything permanent, and that's okay. But I…"

The matter-of-fact statement surprised him. "What do you mean, I don't want anything permanent?"

"I mean, you aren't a marrying man."

He looked puzzled. He smiled slowly. "Leslie, you're a virgin," he said softly.

"I know that's a drawback, but we all have to start somewhere. You can teach me how," she said stubbornly. "I can learn."

"No!" he said softly. "It's not that at all." His eyes seemed to flicker and then burn like black coals. "Leslie, I don't play around with virgins."

Her mind wasn't getting this at all. She felt dazed by her own desire. "You don't?"

"No, I don't," he said firmly.

"Well, if you'll cooperate, I won't be one for much longer," she pointed out. "So there goes your last argument, Matt." She pressed deliberately closer to him, as aware as he was that his body was amazingly capable.

He actually flushed. He pushed away from her and moved her back into her own seat firmly, pulling up the straps of her dress with hands that fumbled a little. He looked as if she'd hit him in the head with something hard.

Puzzled, she fiddled with her seat belt as he snapped his own into place.

He looked formidably upset. He started the car with subdued violence and put it in gear, his expression hard and stoic.

As the Jaguar shot forward, she slanted a glance at him. It puzzled her that he'd backed away from her. Surely he wasn't insulted by her offer? Or maybe he was.

"Are you offended?" she asked, suddenly self-conscious and embarrassed.

"Heavens, no!" he exclaimed.

"Okay." She let out a relieved sigh. She glanced

at him. He wouldn't look at her. "Are you sure you aren't?"

He nodded.

She wrapped her arms around her chest and stared out the windshield at the darkened landscape, trying to decide why he was acting so strangely. He certainly wasn't the man she thought she knew. She'd been certain that he wanted her, too. Now she wasn't.

The Jaguar purred along and they rode in silence. He didn't speak or look at her. He seemed to be deep in thought and she wondered if she'd ruined their budding relationship for good with her wanton tendencies.

It wasn't until he turned the car down a dirt road a few miles from the ranch that she realized he wasn't going toward the Ballengers' home.

"Where are we?" she asked when he turned down an even narrower dirt road that led to a lake. Signposts pointed to various cabins, one of which had Caldwell on it. He pulled into the yard of a little wood cabin in the woods, facing the lake, and cut off the engine.

"This is where I come to get away from business," he told her bluntly. "I've never brought a woman here."

"You haven't?"

His eyes narrowed on her flushed face. "You said you wanted to find out if you could function intimately. All right. We have a place where we won't be disturbed, and I'm willing. More than willing. So there's no reason to be embarrassed,'' he said quietly. ''I want you every bit as badly as you want me. I have something to use. There won't be any risk. But you have to be sure this is what you really want. Once I take your virginity, I can't give it back. There's only one first time.''

She stared at him. Her whole body felt hot at the way he was looking at her. She remembered the feel of his mouth on her breasts and her lips parted hungrily. But it was more than just hunger. He knew it.

She lifted her face to his and brushed a breathless little kiss against his firm chin. ''I wouldn't let any other man touch me,'' she said quietly. ''And I think you know it.''

''Yes. I know it.'' He knew something else as well; he knew that it was going to be a beginning, not an affair or a one-night stand. He was going to be her first man, but she was going to be his last woman. She was all he wanted in the world.

He got out and led her up the steps on to the wide porch where there was a swing and three rocking chairs. He unlocked the door, ushered her inside and locked it again. Taking her hand in his, he led her to the bedroom in back. There was a huge king-size bed in the room. It was covered by a thick comforter in shades of beige and red.

For the first time since she'd been so brazen with him, reality hit her like a cold cloth. She stood just inside the doorway, her eyes riveted on that bed, as erotic pictures of Matt without clothing danced in her thoughts.

He turned to her, backing her up against the closed door. He sensed her nervousness, her sudden uncertainty.

"Are you afraid?" he asked somberly.

"I'm sorry, I guess I am," she said with a forced smile.

His lean hands framed her face and he bent and kissed her eyelids. "This may be your first time. It isn't mine. By the time we end up on that bed, you'll be ready for me, and fear is the very last thing you're going to feel."

He bent to her mouth then and began to kiss her. The caresses were tender and slow, not arousing. If anything, they comforted. She felt her fear of him, of the unknown, melt away like ice in the hot sun. After a few seconds, she relaxed and gave in to his gentle ardor.

At first it was just pleasant. Then she felt him move closer and his body reacted at once to hers.

He caught his breath as he felt the sudden surge of pleasure.

Her hands smoothed up his hard thighs, savoring the muscular warmth of them while his mouth captured hers and took possession of it a little roughly, because she was intensifying the desire that was already consuming him.

His body began to move on her, slow and caressing, arousing and tantalizing. Her breasts felt heavy.

Her nipples were taut, and the friction of the silky cloth against them intensified the sensations he was kindling in her body, the desire she was already feeling.

His knee edged between both her legs in the silky dress and the slow movement of his hips made her body clench.

His hands went between them, working deftly on the tiny straps of her dress while he kissed her. It wasn't until she felt the rough hair of his chest against her bare breasts that she realized both of them were uncovered from the waist up.

He drew away a little and looked down at her firm, pretty little breasts while he traced them with his fingers.

"I'd like to keep you under lock and key," he murmured gruffly. "My own pretty little treasure," he added as his head bent.

She watched his mouth take her, felt the pleasure of warm lips on her body. She liked the sight of his mouth over her nipple, that dark, wavy hair falling unruly onto his broad forehead while his heavy eyebrows met and his eyes closed under the delicious whip of passion. She held his head to her body, smoothing the hair at his nape, feeling it cool and clean under her fingers.

When he finally lifted his head, she was leaning back against the door for support. Her eyes were misty with desire, her body trembled faintly with the force of it. She looked at him hungrily, with all the barriers down at last. Other men might repulse her, but she wanted Matt. She loved the feel of his hands and his eyes and his mouth on her body. She wanted to lie under him and feel the delicious pressure of his body against and over and inside her own. She wanted it so badly that she moaned softly.

"No second thoughts?" he asked gently.

"Oh, no! No second thoughts, Matt," she whispered, adoring him with her eyes.

With a slow, secret smile, he began to divest her of the dress and the remaining piece of clothing, leaving her standing before him with her body unveiled, taut with passion.

She was shy, but his hands soon made a jumble of her embarrassment. She felt her body jerk rhythmically as he suckled her breasts. It was so sweet. It was paradise.

When he eased her down onto the huge bed, she lay back against the pillows, totally yielding, and watched his evening clothes come off little by little. He watched her while he undressed, laughing softly, a sensual predatory note in his deep voice. She moved helplessly on the coverlet, her entire being aflame with sensations she'd never known. She could barely wait. She felt as if she was throbbing all over, burning with some unknown fire that threatened to consume her, an ache that was almost painful.

Her eyes widened when the last piece of fabric came away from his powerful body and her breath caught.

He liked that expression. He turned away just for a minute, long enough to extricate a packet from his wallet. He sat down beside her, opened it, and taught her matter-of-factly what to do with it. She fumbled a little, her eyes incredibly wide and fascinated and a little frightened.

"I won't hurt you," he said gently, searching her eyes. "Women have been doing this for hundreds of thousands of years. You're going to like it, Leslie. I promise you are."

She lay back, watching him with wide gray eyes full of curiosity as he slid alongside her.

His dark head bent to her body and she lay under him like a creamy, blushing sacrifice, learning the different ways she responded to his touch. He laughed when she arched up and moaned. He liked the way she opened to him, the way her breath rasped when his mouth slid tenderly over her belly and the soft, inner skin of her thighs. He made a sensual meal of her there on the pretty, soft comforter, while the sound of rain came closer outside the window, the moonlit night clouding over as a storm moved above the cabin.

She hadn't known that physical pleasure could be so devastating. She watched him touch and taste her, with eyes equally fascinated and aroused by some of the things he did to her.

Her shocked exclamation pulled an amused laugh from him. "Am I shocking you? Don't you read books and watch movies?'' he asked as he poised just above her.

"It isn't...the same," she choked, arching as his body began to tease hers, her long legs shifting eagerly out of his way as he moved down against her.

Her hands were clenched beside her head, and he watched her eyes dilate as his hips shifted tenderly and she felt him against her in a shattering new intimacy. She gasped, looking straight into his dark eyes. "I...never dreamed...!"

"No words on earth could describe how this feels," he murmured, his breath rasping as he hesitated and then moved down again, tenderly. "You're beautiful, Leslie. Your body is exquisite, soft and warm and enticing. I love the way your skin feels under my mouth." His breath caught as he moved closer and felt her body protest at the invasion. He paused to search over her flushed, drawn face. "I'm becoming your lover," he whispered huskily, drawing his body against hers sensuously to deepen his possession. "I'm going inside you. Now."

His face became rigid with control, solemn as he met her eyes and pushed again, harder, and watched her flinch. "I know. It's going to hurt a little, in spite of everything," he said softly. "But not for long. Do you still want me?"

"More than anything...in the world!" she choked, lifting her hips toward his in a sensual invitation. "It's all right." She swallowed. Impulsively she looked down and her mouth fell open. She couldn't have imagined watching, even a day before. "Matt...!" she gasped.

Her eyes came back up to his. His face looked as if every muscle in it was clenched. "It feels like my first time, too," he said a little roughly. His hands slid under her head, cradling it as he shifted slightly and then pushed once more.

Her pretty body lifted off the bed. It seemed to ripple as he moved intimately into closer contact. "I never thought...we could talk...while we did something so intimate," she whispered back, gasping when he moved again and pleasure shot through her. "Yes...oh, yes, please do...that!" she pleaded huskily, clutching at his shoulders.

"Here, like this?" he asked urgently, and moved again.

Her tiny cry was affirmation enough. He eased down on her, his eyes looking straight into hers as he began a rhythm that combined tension with exquisite pleasure and fleeting, burning pain.

His eyes dilated as he felt the barrier. He shivered. His body clenched. He'd never had an innocent woman. Leslie was totally out of his experience. He hadn't thought about how it would feel until now. Primitive thoughts claimed his mind, ancestral memories perhaps that spoke of an ancient age when this would have been a rite of passage.

She was feeling something very similar as her body yielded to the domination of his. The discomfort paled beside the feelings that were consuming her. Glimpses of unbelievable pleasure were mingling with the stinging pain. Past it, she knew, lay ecstasy.

He kissed her hungrily as his lean, fit body moved on her in the silence of the cabin. Suddenly rain pounded hard outside the curtained window, slamming into the roof, the ground, the trees. The wind howled around the corner. There was a storm in him, too, as he lay stretched tight with desire, trying to hold back long enough to let Leslie share what he knew he would feel.

"I've never been so hungry," he bit off against her mouth. His hands contracted under her head, tangling in her hair. His body shuddered. "I'm going to have to hurt you. I can't wait any longer. It's getting away from me. I have to have you…now!"

Her legs moved sensuously against his, loving the faint abrasion of the hair that covered his. "Yes!" she said huskily, her eyes full of wonder. "I want it. I want…it with you."

One lean hand went to her upper thigh. His lips flattened. He looked straight into her eyes as his hand suddenly pinned her hips and he thrust down fiercely.

She cried out, grimacing, writhing as she felt him deep in her body, past a stinging pain that engulfed her.

He stilled, holding her in place while he gave her body time to adjust, his eyes blazing with primitive triumph. His gaze reflected pride and pleasure and possession.

"Yes," he said roughly. "You're part of me and I'm part of you. Now you belong to me, completely."

Her eyes mirrored her shocked fascination. She moved a little and felt him move with her. She swallowed, and then swallowed again, her breath coming in soft jerks as she adjusted to her first intimacy. She loved him. The feel of him was pure delight. She was a woman. She could be a woman. The past was dying already and she was whole and sensuous and fully capable. Her smile was brilliant with joyful self-discovery.

She pulled his head down to hers and kissed him hungrily. The pain had receded and now she felt a new sensation as his hips moved. There were tiny little spasms of pleasure. Her breath came raggedly as she positioned herself to hold on to them. Her nails bit into the hard muscle of his upper arms.

His dark eyes were full of indulgent amusement as he felt her movements. She hesitated once, shy. "Don't stop," he whispered. "I'll do whatever you want me to do."

Her lips parted. It wasn't the answer she'd expected.

He bent and kissed her eyelids again, his breath growing more ragged by the minute. "Find a position that gives you what you need," he coaxed. "I won't take my pleasure until you've had yours."

"Oh, Matt," she moaned, unbearably touched by a generosity that she hadn't expected.

He laughed through his desire, kissing her face tenderly. "My own treasure," he whispered. "I wish I could make it last for hours. I want you to blush when you're sixty, remembering this first time. I want it to be perfect for you."

The pleasure was building. It was fierce now, and she was no longer in control of her own body. It lifted up to Matt's and demanded pleasure. She was totally at the mercy of her awakened passion, blind with the need for fulfillment. She became aware of a new sort of tension that was lifting her fiercely to meet every quick, downward motion of his lean hips, that stretched her under his powerful body, that made her pulse leap with delicious throbs of wild delight.

He watched her body move and ripple, watched the expression on her face, in her wide, blind eyes, and smiled. "Yes," he murmured to himself. "Now you understand, don't you? You can't fight it, or deny it, or control it..." He stopped abruptly.

"No! Please, don't...stop!" Her choked cry was followed by frantic, clinging hands that pulled at him.

He eased down again, watching as she shivered. "I'm not going to stop," he whispered softly. "Trust me. I only want to make it as good as it can be for you."

"It feels...wonderful," she said hoarsely. "Every time you move, it's like...like electric shocks of pleasure."

"And we've barely started, baby," he whispered.

He shifted his hips, intensifying her cries. She was completely yielded to him, open to him, wanton. He'd never dreamed that it would be like this. His head began to spin with the delight his body was taking from hers.

She curled her long legs around his powerful ones and lifted herself, gasping when it brought a sharp stab of pleasure.

His hand swept down her body. His face hardened as he began to increase the pressure and the rhythm. She clung to him, her mouth in his throat, on his chest, his chin, wherever she could reach, while he gave in to his fierce hunger and threw away his control.

She'd never dreamed how it would be. She couldn't get close enough, or hold on tight enough. She felt him in every cell of her body. She was ardent, inciting him, matching his quick, hard movements, her back lifting to promote an even closer contact.

She whispered things to him, secret, erotic things that drove him to sensual urgency. She was moaning. She could hear her frantic voice pleading, hear the sound their movements made on the box springs, feel the power and heat of him as her body opened for him and clenched with tension that begged for release.

She whispered his name and then groaned it, and then repeated it in a mad, hoarse little sound until the little throbs of pleasure became one long, aching,

endless spasm of ecstasy that made her blind and
deaf under the fierce, demanding thrust of his body.
She cried out and shivered in the grip of it, her voice
throbbing like her body. She felt herself go off the
edge of the world into space, into a red heat that
washed over every cell in her body.

When she was able to think again, she felt his
body shake violently, heard the harsh groan at her
ear as he, too, found ecstasy.

He shuddered one last time and then his warm
strong body relaxed and she felt it push hers deeper
into the mattress. His mouth was at her throat, pressing hungrily. His lips moved all over her face, touching and lifting in a fever of tenderness.

Her dazed eyes opened and looked up into his. He
was damp with sweat, as she was. His dark eyes
smiled with incredible gentleness into hers.

She arched helplessly and moaned as the pleasure
washed over her again.

"More?" he whispered, and his hips moved oblig-
ingly, so that the sweet stabs of delight came again
and again and again.

She sobbed helplessly afterward, clinging to him
as she lay against his relaxed body.

His hand smoothed over her damp hair. He seemed
to understand her shattered response, as she didn't.

"I don't know why I'm bawling my head off,"
she choked, "when it was the closest to heaven I've
ever been."

"There are half a dozen technical names for it,"

he murmured drowsily. "It's letdown blues. You go so high that it hurts to come down."

"I went high," she murmured with a smile. "I walked on the moon."

He chuckled. "So did I."

"Was...was it all right?" she asked suddenly.

He rolled her over on her back and looked down into her curious face. "You were the best lover I've ever had," he said, and he wasn't teasing. "And you will be, from now on, the only woman I ever have."

"Oh, that sounds serious," she murmured.

"Doesn't it, though?" His dark eyes went over her like an artist's brush committing beauty to canvas. He touched her soft breasts with a breathlessly tender caress. "I won't be able to stop, you know," he added conversationally.

"Stop?"

"This," he replied. "It's addictive. Now that I've had you, I'll want you all the time. I'll go green every time any other man so much as looks at you."

It sounded as if he was trying to tell her something, and she couldn't decide what it was. She searched his dark eyes intently.

He smiled with indulgent affection. "Do you want the words?"

"Which words?" she whispered.

He brushed his lips over hers with incredible, breathless tenderness. "Marry me, Leslie."

Chapter Thirteen

Her gasp was audible. It was more than she'd dared hope for when she came in here with him. He chuckled at her expression.

"Did you think I was going to ask you to come out to the ranch and live in sin with me?" he teased with twinkling eyes. His hand swept down over her body possessively. "This isn't enough. Not nearly enough."

She hesitated. "Are you sure that you want something, well, permanent?"

His eyes narrowed. "Leslie, if I'd been a little more reckless, you'd have something permanent. I wanted very badly to make you pregnant."

Her face brightened. "Did you, really? I thought about it, too, just at the end."

He smoothed back her hair and found himself fighting the temptation to start all over again with nothing between them.

"We'll have children," he promised her. "But first we'll build a life together, a secure life that they'll fall into very naturally."

She was fascinated by the expression on his face. It was only just dawning on her that he felt more than a fleeting desire for her body. He was talking about a life together, children together. She knew very little about true relationships, but she was learning all the time.

"Heavy thoughts?" he teased.

"Yes." She smoothed her fingers over his lean cheek.

"Care to share them?" he murmured.

"I was thinking how sweet it is to be loved," she whispered softly.

He lifted an eyebrow. "Physically loved?"

"Well, that, too," she replied.

He smiled quizzically. "Too?"

"You'd never have taken me to bed unless you loved me," she said simply, but with conviction. "You have these strange old-world hang-ups about innocence."

"Strange, my foot!"

She smiled up at him complacently. "Not that I don't like them," she assured him. The smile faded as she searched his dark eyes. "It was perfect. Just perfect. And I'm glad I waited for you. I love you, Matt.''

His chest rose and fell heavily. ''Even after the way I've treated you?''

''You didn't know the truth,'' she said. ''And even if you were unfair at first, you made all sorts of restitution. I won't have a limp anymore,'' she added, wide-eyed. ''And you gave me a good job and looked out for me...''

He bent and kissed her hungrily. ''Don't try to make it sound better than it was. I've been an ogre with you. I'm only sorry that I can't go back and start over again.''

''None of us can do that,'' she said. ''But we have a second chance, both of us. That's something to be thankful for.''

''From now on,'' he promised her solemnly, ''everything is going to be just the way you want it. The past has been hard for me to overcome. I've distrusted women for so long, but with you I've been able to forget what my mother did. I'll cherish you as long as I live.''

''And I'll cherish you,'' she replied quietly. ''I thought I would never know what it was to be loved.''

He frowned a little, drawing her palm to his lips. ''I never thought I would, either. I was never in love before.''

She sighed tenderly. ''Neither was I. And I never dreamed it would be so sweet.''

"I imagine it's going to get better year after year," he ventured, toying with her fingers.

Her free hand slid up into his dark hair. "Matt?"

"What?"

"Can we do that again?"

He pursed his lips. "Are you sure that you can?" he asked pointedly.

She shifted on the coverlet and grimaced with the movement. "Well, maybe not. Oh, dear."

He actually laughed, bending to wrap her up against him and kiss her with rough affection. "Come here, walking wounded. We'll have a nice nap and then we'll go home and make wedding plans." He smoothed down her wild hair. "We'll have a nice cozy wedding and a honeymoon anywhere you want to go."

"I don't mind if we don't go anywhere, as long as I'm with you," she said honestly.

He sighed. "My thoughts exactly." He glanced down at her. "You could have had a conventional wedding night, you know."

She smoothed her hand over his hair-roughened chest. "I didn't know that you'd want to marry me. But just the same, I had to know if I could function intimately with you. I wasn't sure, you see."

"I am," he said with a wicked grin.

She laughed heartily. "Yes, so am I, now, but it was important that I knew the truth before things went any further between us. I knew it was difficult for you to hold back, and I couldn't bear the thought of letting you go. Not that I expected you to want to marry me,'' she added ruefully.

''I wanted to marry you the first time I kissed you,'' he confessed. ''Not to mention the first time I danced with you. It was magic.''

''For me, too.''

''But you had this strange aversion to me and I couldn't understand why. I was a beast to you. Even Ed said it wasn't like me to treat employees that badly. He read me the riot act and I let him.''

''Ed's nice.''

''He is. But I'm glad you weren't in love with him. At first, I couldn't be sure of the competition.''

''Ed was a brotherly sort. He still is.'' She kissed his chest. ''But I love you.''

''I love you, too.''

She laid her cheek against the place she'd kissed and closed her eyes. ''If the lawyers can help my mother, maybe she'll be out for the first christening.''

''At least for the second,'' he agreed, and smiled as his arms closed warm and protective around her, drawing her closer. It was the safest she'd ever been in her life, in those warm, strong arms in the darkness. The nightmares seemed to fade into the shadows of reality that they'd become. She would walk in the light, now, unafraid. The past was over, truly over. She knew that it would never torment her again.

Matt and Leslie were married in the local Presbyterian church, and the pews were full all the way to the back. Leslie thought that every single inhabitant of Jacobsville had shown up for the wedding, and she wasn't far wrong. Matt Caldwell had been the town's foremost bachelor for so long that curiosity brought people for miles around. All the Hart boys showed up, including the state attorney general, as well as the Ballengers, the Tremaynes, the Jacobs, the Coltrains, the Deverells, the Regans and the Burkes. The turnout read like the local social register.

Leslie wore a white designer gown with a long train and oceans of veiling and lace. The women in the office served as maids and matrons of honor, and Luke Craig acted as Matt's best man. There were flower girls and a concert pianist. The local press was invited, but no out of town reporters. Nobody wrote about Leslie's tragic past, either. It was a beautiful ceremony and the reception was uproarious.

Matt had pushed back her veil at the altar with the look of a man who'd inherited heaven. He smiled as he bent to kiss her, and his eyes were soft with love, as were her own.

They held hands all through the noisy reception on the lawn at Matt's ranch, where barbecue was the order of the day.

Leslie had already changed clothes and was walking among the guests when she came upon Carolyn Engles unexpectedly.

The beautiful blonde came right up to her with a genuine smile and a present in her hands.

"I got this for you, in Paris," Carolyn said with visible hesitation and self-consciousness. "It's sort of a peace offering and an apology, all in one."

"You didn't have to do this," Leslie stammered.

"I did." She nodded toward the silver-wrapped present. "Open it."

Leslie pulled off the paper with helpless excitement, puzzled and touched by the other woman's gesture. She opened the velvet box inside and her breath caught. It was a beautiful little crystal swan, tiny and perfect.

"I thought it was a nice analogy," Carolyn murmured. "You've turned out to be a lovely swan, and nobody's going to hurt you when you go swimming around in the Jacobsville pond."

Impulsively Leslie hugged the older woman, who laughed nervously and actually blushed.

"I'm sorry for what I did that day," Carolyn said huskily. "Really sorry. I had no idea…"

"I don't hold grudges," Leslie said gently.

"I know that." She shrugged. "I was infatuated with Matt and he couldn't see me for dust. I went a little crazy, but I'm myself again now. I want you both to be very happy."

"I hope the same for you," Leslie said with a smile.

Matt saw them together and frowned. He came up beside Leslie and placed an arm around her protectively.

"Carolyn brought this to me from Paris," Leslie

said excitedly, showing him the tiny thing. "Isn't it beautiful?"

Matt was obviously puzzled as he exchanged looks with Carolyn.

"I'm not as bad as you think I am," Carolyn told him. "I really do hope you'll be happy. Both of you."

Matt's eyes smiled. "Thank you."

Carolyn smiled back ruefully. "I told Leslie how sorry I was for the way I behaved. I really am, Matt."

"We all have periods of lunacy," Matt replied. "Otherwise, nobody in his right mind would ever get into the cattle business."

Carolyn laughed delightedly. "So they say. I have to go. I just wanted to bring Leslie the peace offering. You'll both be on my guest list for the charity ball, by the way."

"We'll come, and thank you," Matt returned.

Carolyn nodded, smiled and moved away toward where the guests' cars were parked.

Matt pulled his new wife closer. "Surprises are breaking out like measles."

"I noticed." She linked her arms around his neck and reached up to kiss him tenderly. "When everybody goes home, we can lock ourselves in the bedroom and play doctor."

He chuckled delightedly. "Can we, now? Who gets to go first?"

"Wait and see!"

He turned her back toward their guests with a grin that went from ear to ear. "Lucky me," he said, and he wasn't joking.

They woke the next morning in a tangle of arms and legs as the sun peered in through the gauzy curtains. Matt's ardor had been inexhaustible, and Leslie had discovered a whole new world of sensation.

She rolled over onto her back and stretched, uninhibited by her nudity. Matt propped himself on an elbow and looked at her with eyes full of love and possession.

"I never realized that marriage would have so many fringe benefits," she murmured. She stretched again. "I don't know if I have enough strength to walk after last night."

"If you don't, I'll carry you," he said with a loving smile. He reached over to kiss her lazily. "Come on, treasure. We'll have a nice shower and then we'll go and find some breakfast."

She kissed him back. "I love you."

"Same here."

"You aren't sorry you married me, are you?" she asked impulsively. "I mean, the past never really goes away. Someday some other reporter may dig it all back up again."

"It won't matter," he said. "Everybody's got a skeleton or two. And no, I'm not sorry I married you. It was the first sensible thing I've done in years. Not to mention,'' he added with a sensual touch of his mouth to her body, "the most pleasurable.''

She laughed. "For me, too.'' Her arms pulled him down to her and she kissed him heartily.

Her mother did get a new trial, and her sentence was shortened. She went back to serve the rest of her time with a light heart, looking forward to the day when she could get to know her daughter all over again.

As for Leslie, she and Matt grew closer with every passing day and became known locally as "the love-birds,'' because they were so rarely seen apart.

Matt's prediction about her mother's release came true as well. Three years after the birth of their son, Leslie gave birth to a daughter who had Matt's dark hair and, he mused, a temper to match his own. He had to fight tears when the baby was placed in his arms. He loved his son, but he'd wanted a little girl who looked like his own treasure, Leslie. Now, he told her, his life was complete. She echoed that sentiment with all her heart. The past had truly been laid to rest. She and Matt had years of happiness ahead of them.

Most of Jacobsville showed up for the baby's christening, including a small blond woman who was enjoying her first days of freedom. Leslie's mother had pride of place in the front pew. Leslie looked from Matt to her mother, from their three-year-old son to the baby in her arms. Her gray eyes, when they lifted to Matt's soft, dark ones, were radiant with joy. Dreams came true, she thought. Dreams came true.

* * * * *

The SOLDIERS OF FORTUNE *are back!*
Don't miss a chance to revisit these
unforgettable romantic classics in a wonderful
3-in-1 keepsake collection
by bestselling author Diana Palmer,
available in April from Silhouette Books.

And if you can't get enough of these
passionate and adventurous stories,
coming your way are all new
SOLDIERS OF FORTUNE *tales.*
This May, Silhouette Romance presents the
next book in this riveting series:

MERCENARY'S WOMAN
by Diana Palmer

She was in danger and he fought to protect
her. But sweet-natured Sally Johnson dreamt
of spending forever in Ebenezer Scott's
powerful embrace. Would she walk down the
aisle as this tender mercenary's bride?
Soldiers of Fortune…prisoners of love.

Celebrate Silhouette's 20th Anniversary

With beloved authors, exciting new miniseries and special keepsake collections, **plus** the chance to enter our 20th anniversary contest, in which one lucky reader wins the trip of a lifetime!

Take a look at who's celebrating with us:

DIANA PALMER

April 2000: SOLDIERS OF FORTUNE
May 2000 in Silhouette Romance: *Mercenary's Woman*

NORA ROBERTS

May 2000: IRISH HEARTS, the 2-in-1 keepsake collection
June 2000 in Special Edition: *Irish Rebel*

LINDA HOWARD

July 2000: MACKENZIE'S MISSION
August 2000 in Intimate Moments: *A Game of Chance*

ANNETTE BROADRICK

October 2000: a special keepsake collection, plus a brand-new title in
November 2000 in Desire

Available at your favorite retail outlet.

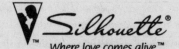

Silhouette®
Where love comes alive™

If you enjoyed what you just read,
then we've got an offer you can't resist!

Take 2 bestselling
love stories FREE!
Plus get a FREE surprise gift!

Clip this page and mail it to Silhouette Reader Service™

IN U.S.A.
3010 Walden Ave.
P.O. Box 1867
Buffalo, N.Y. 14240-1867

IN CANADA
P.O. Box 609
Fort Erie, Ontario
L2A 5X3

YES! Please send me 2 free Silhouette Special Edition® novels and my free surprise gift. Then send me 6 brand-new novels every month, which I will receive months before they're available in stores. In the U.S.A., bill me at the bargain price of $3.57 plus 25¢ delivery per book and applicable sales tax, if any*. In Canada, bill me at the bargain price of $3.96 plus 25¢ delivery per book and applicable taxes**. That's the complete price and a savings of over 10% off the cover prices—what a great deal! I understand that accepting the 2 free books and gift places me under no obligation ever to buy any books. I can always return a shipment and cancel at any time. Even if I never buy another book from Silhouette, the 2 free books and gift are mine to keep forever. So why not take us up on our invitation. You'll be glad you did!

235 SEN CNFD
335 SEN CNFE

_____

Name   (PLEASE PRINT)

_____

Address   Apt.#

_____

City   State/Prov.   Zip/Postal Code

* Terms and prices subject to change without notice. Sales tax applicable in N.Y.
** Canadian residents will be charged applicable provincial taxes and GST.
   All orders subject to approval. Offer limited to one per household.
   ® are registered trademarks of Harlequin Enterprises Limited.

SPED99   ©1998 Harlequin Enterprises Limited

MONTANA MAVERICKS
Big Sky Brides

Legendary love comes to Whitehorn, Montana,
once more as beloved authors

Christine Rimmer, Jennifer Greene and Cheryl St.John

present three brand-new stories in this exciting anthology!

Meet the Brennan women:
SUZANNA, DIANA and ISABELLE

Strong-willed beauties who find unexpected
love in these irresistible marriage of
covnenience stories.

Don't miss
MONTANA MAVERICKS: BIG SKY BRIDES
On sale in February 2000,
only from Silhouette Books!

Available at your favorite retail outlet.

Silhouette®

SILHOUETTE'S 20ᵀᴴ ANNIVERSARY CONTEST
OFFICIAL RULES
NO PURCHASE NECESSARY TO ENTER

1. To enter, follow directions published in the offer to which you are responding. Contest begins 1/1/00 and ends on 8/24/00 (the "Promotion Period"). Method of entry may vary. Mailed entries must be postmarked by 8/24/00, and received by 8/31/00.

2. During the Promotion Period, the Contest may be presented via the Internet. Entry via the Internet may be restricted to residents of certain geographic areas that are disclosed on the Web site. To enter via the Internet, if you are a resident of a geographic area in which Internet entry is permissible, follow the directions displayed on-line, including typing your essay of 100 words or fewer telling us "Where In The World Your Love Will Come Alive." On-line entries must be received by 11:59 p.m. Eastern Standard time on 8/24/00. Limit one e-mail entry per person, household and e-mail address per day, per presentation. If you are a resident of a geographic area in which entry via the Internet is permissible, you may, in lieu of submitting an entry on-line, enter by mail, by hand-printing your name, address, telephone number and contest number/name on an 8"x 11" plain piece of paper and telling us in 100 words or fewer "Where In The World Your Love Will Come Alive," and mailing via first-class mail to: Silhouette 20ᵗʰ Anniversary Contest, (in the U.S.) P.O. Box 9069, Buffalo, NY 14269-9069; (In Canada) P.O. Box 637, Fort Erie, Ontario, Canada L2A 5X3. Limit one 8"x 11" mailed entry per person, household and e-mail address per day. On-line and/or 8"x 11" mailed entries received from persons residing in geographic areas in which Internet entry is not permissible will be disqualified. No liability is assumed for lost, late, incomplete, inaccurate, nondelivered or misdirected mail, or misdirected e-mail, for technical, hardware or software failures of any kind, lost or unavailable network connection, or failed, incomplete, garbled or delayed computer transmission or any human error which may occur in the receipt or processing of the entries in the contest.

3. Essays will be judged by a panel of members of the Silhouette editorial and marketing staff based on the following criteria:

> Sincerity (believability, credibility)—50%
> Originality (freshness, creativity)—30%
> Aptness (appropriateness to contest ideas)—20%

Purchase or acceptance of a product offer does not improve your chances of winning. In the event of a tie, duplicate prizes will be awarded.

4. All entries become the property of Harlequin Enterprises Ltd., and will not be returned. Winner will be determined no later than 10/31/00 and will be notified by mail. Grand Prize winner will be required to sign and return Affidavit of Eligibility within 15 days of receipt of notification. Noncompliance within the time period may result in disqualification and an alternative winner may be selected. All municipal, provincial, federal, state and local laws and regulations apply. Contest open only to residents of the U.S. and Canada who are 18 years of age or older, and is void wherever prohibited by law. Internet entry is restricted solely to residents of those geographical areas in which Internet entry is permissible. Employees of Torstar Corp., their affiliates, agents and members of their immediate families are not eligible. Taxes on the prizes are the sole responsibility of winners. Entry and acceptance of any prize offered constitutes permission to use winner's name, photograph or other likeness for the purposes of advertising, trade and promotion on behalf of Torstar Corp. without further compensation to the winner, unless prohibited by law. Torstar Corp and D.L. Blair, Inc., their parents, affiliates and subsidiaries, are not responsible for errors in printing or electronic presentation of contest or entries. In the event of printing or other errors which may result in unintended prize values or duplication of prizes, all affected contest materials or entries shall be null and void. If for any reason the Internet portion of the contest is not capable of running as planned, including infection by computer virus, bugs, tampering, unauthorized intervention, fraud, technical failures, or any other causes beyond the control of Torstar Corp. which corrupt or affect the administration, secrecy, fairness, integrity or proper conduct of the contest, Torstar Corp. reserves the right, at its sole discretion, to disqualify any individual who tampers with the entry process and to cancel, terminate, modify or suspend the contest or the Internet portion thereof. In the event of a dispute regarding an on-line entry, the entry will be deemed submitted by the authorized holder of the e-mail account submitted at the time of entry. Authorized account holder is defined as the natural person who is assigned to an e-mail address by an Internet access provider, on-line service provider or other organization that is responsible for arranging e-mail address for the domain associated with the submitted e-mail address.

5. Prizes: Grand Prize—a $10,000 vacation to anywhere in the world. Travelers (at least one must be 18 years of age or older) or parent or guardian if one traveler is a minor, must sign and return a Release of Liability prior to departure. Travel must be completed by December 31, 2001, and is subject to space and accommodations availability. Two hundred (200) Second Prizes—a two-book limited edition autographed collector set from one of the Silhouette Anniversary authors: Nora Roberts, Diana Palmer, Linda Howard or Annette Broadrick (value $10.00 each set). All prizes are valued in U.S. dollars.

6. For a list of winners (available after 10/31/00), send a self-addressed, stamped envelope to: Harlequin Silhouette 20ᵗʰ Anniversary Winners, P.O. Box 4200, Blair, NE 68009-4200.

Contest sponsored by Torstar Corp., P.O. Box 9042, Buffalo, NY 14269-9042.

ENTER FOR
A CHANCE TO WIN*

Silhouette's 20th Anniversary Contest

Tell Us Where in the World
You Would Like *Your* Love To Come Alive...
And We'll Send the Lucky Winner There!

Silhouette wants to take you wherever
your happy ending can come true.

Here's how to enter: Tell us, in 100 words or less,
where you want to go to make your love come alive!

In addition to the grand prize, there will be 200
runner-up prizes, collector's-edition book sets
autographed by one of the Silhouette anniversary
authors: **Nora Roberts, Diana Palmer,
Linda Howard** or **Annette Broadrick**.

DON'T MISS YOUR CHANCE TO WIN!
ENTER NOW! No Purchase Necessary

Silhouette®
Where love comes alive™

Name:

Address:

City: State/Province:

Zip/Postal Code:

Mail to Harlequin Books: **In the U.S.**: P.O. Box 9069, Buffalo, NY
14269-9069; **In Canada**: P.O. Box 637, Fort Erie, Ontario, L4A 5X3

*No purchase necessary—for contest details send a self-addressed stamped envelope to:
Silhouette's 20th Anniversary Contest, P.O. Box 9069, Buffalo, NY, 14269-9069 (include
contest name on self-addressed envelope). Residents of Washington and Vermont may
omit postage. Open to Cdn. (excluding Quebec) and U.S. residents who are 18 or over.
Void where prohibited. Contest ends August 31, 2000.

PS20CON_R

Silhouette®

SPECIAL EDITION

COMING NEXT MONTH

#1303 MAN...MERCENARY...MONARCH—Joan Elliott Pickart
Royally Wed
In the blink of an eye, John Colton discovered he was a Crown Prince, a
brand-new father...and a man on the verge of falling for a woman in *his*
royal family's employ. Yet trust—and love—didn't come easily to this
one-time mercenary who desperately wanted to be son, brother,
father...*husband?*

#1304 DR. MOM AND THE MILLIONAIRE—Christine Flynn
Prescription: Marriage
No woman had been able to get the powerful Chase Harrington anywhere
near an altar. Then again, this confirmed bachelor had never met someone
like the charmingly fascinating Dr. Alexandra Larson, a woman whose
tender loving care promised to heal him, body, heart...and soul.

#1305 WHO'S THAT BABY?—Diana Whitney
So Many Babies
Johnny Winterhawk did what any red-blooded male would when he found
a baby on his doorstep—he panicked. Pediatrician Claire Davis rescued
him by offering her hand in a marriage of convenience...and then showed
him just how real a family they could be.

#1306 CATTLEMAN'S COURTSHIP—Lois Faye Dyer
Experience made Quinn Bowdrie a tough man of the land who didn't need
anybody. That is, until he met the sweetly tempting Victoria Denning, the
only woman who could teach this stubborn rancher the pleasures of
courtship.

#1307 THE MARRIAGE BASKET—Sharon De Vita
The Blackwell Brothers
Rina Roberts had her heart set on adopting her orphaned nephew. But the
boy's godfather, Hunter Blackwell, stood in her way. Their love for the
child drew them together and Rina knew that not only did the handsome
doctor hold the key to Billy's future—but also to her own heart.

#1308 FALLING FOR AN OLDER MAN—Trisha Alexander
Callahans & Kin
Sheila Callahan dreamed of picket fences and wedding rings, but
Jack Kinsella, the man of her dreams, wasn't the slightest bit interested in
commitment, especially not to his best friend's younger sister. But one
night together created more than just passion....